MsFitZ CAFÉ

BY

JEAN THOMPSON KINSEY

Jean T Kinsey

Copyright by Jean T. Kinsey@2015

MsFitZ CAFE

No part of this book shall be copied or printed without the express permission of the publisher.

All mentioned characters are fictitious and not to be associated with any individuals.

Jean T Kinsey

Dedication:

To Cindy, my other daughter. Thank you for all you do.

To the memory of my dear online friends and writing buddies, Toni Metcalf and Nike Chilemi.

Thank You to Kathy Keller for helping with title and to Diane Theiler, Becky Kelley, Susan Hawthorne, and Betty Thomason Owens for the critiques.

MsFitZ CAFE

Chapter One

Abigail Fitzgerald bit her lower lip. Green neon letters **M- s -F -i -t-Z** C-A-F-E chased each other across the marquee. She nodded. *Appropriate.* Some thought 'misfits' signified her motley crew of employees, but they didn't know all, and she wasn't about to tell them.

Loud barking and the sudden clamor from awaiting yard sale enthusiasts ripped Abby's concentration from the billboard. A huge, gray dog, with drooling jowls headed toward the tables of bakery goods she'd added to other items in the annual benefit sidewalk sale. Christmas for the little ones this year was supposed to be great. A stray dog wouldn't ruin it; not if she could help it. Abby waved her arms and legs jumping-jacks style and shouted, "Get! Get. Get away from here, you mangy critter."

The startled Weimaraner ran under the first table, turning it upside down, and toppled another, yielding a domino effect to the third and fourth. Desserts, multi-colored books, and variegated handmade crafts sailed through the air -- a kaleidoscope of disaster. Sidewalk-bystanders didn't know what to do. Some tried to catch flying pies and cakes but only grabbed handfuls of chocolate, lemon, or fruit. Others retreated out of reach of the messy airborne globs.

"Raney. Raney!" a man called between huffs and puffs as he sprinted across the street, his voice bristly as his stubbly beard. "Stop, Raney. Stop, I say." The canine finally heeded his master's call, sidled up to him, and dropped his head. "Raney, what have you done?"

"Wrecked hundreds of dollars' of my merchandise. That's what he's done." Lips drawn into a fine line and jaws clenched, Abby marched toward them but stepped in the remains of a chocolate pie that sent her feet skidding. Mouth agape, hands frozen in mid-air, her butt landed in the gooey mess.

"I'm so sorry. I'll make this up to you." Raney's master offered his hand to help, and Abby reached up to accept his assistance until a sly, uncontained grin crinkled around the man's lips. Abby retracted her hand with a quick jerk.

Still sitting in her chocolate pie, she scowled at both dog and man. "I don't know which one of you is the more despicable." Raney raised his chocolaty-lemon-covered head with *what did I do wrong?* written in sad, pink eyes.

Two co-workers flew out the café door to their employer's aid. The sassy one with the blond ponytail helped her to her feet. The other quickly bent to swab up some of the goop from Abby's backside, her long black hair falling to hide her face and the remnants of her beautiful Latin laugh she desperately tried to quell. If eyes could shoot cannonballs, both man and his dog would be in terrible pain at that moment.

"Lady, I tried to apologize. If you had not gone into

MsFitZ CAFE

a temper tantrum, I was trying to say I'm sorry and will
pay for the damage." He poked a crisp hundred-dollar bill at her. "A hundred dollars you said? Here take it.
According to that fit you're throwing, you must really
need it."
"I said hundreds of dollars." A tic dimpled Abby's cheek as she snatched the money from his hand. "Before I come up with an exact figure, I'll need to do the math."
According to the gathering crowd, there was just no way to predict the sales she'd lost. Of course, to be honest, a great deal of them were probably here only out of curiosity. Ratty sweatshirt and worn-out jeans. She closed her eyes and sighed. Might as well take the money and call it settled. He probably couldn't afford this hundred. It was possibly the last bit of his Social Security check for the month. A twinge of compassion niggled. Hurting another person to help her girls was not Abby. Money in hand, she stepped forward to return the man's cash.
He grumbled at her, "Tally up your loss and send me
a bill. But don't try to rip me off. I'm nobody's fool."
Abby's face burned hot enough to fry an egg on her cheeks. When. had she ever been so furious? Friends often commented on her tolerance, but this was different. "I'm not the one to whom you owe an apology. Every dime of that money was earmarked to help single moms

and their children with Christmas this year. You know, they're the real losers."

His brow curved into three creased contours, and in a softer tone he said, "No, I didn't know."

Why did he look so familiar? Should she recognize him? Abby used two fingers to pick a chocolate-coated business card from the sidewalk and wiped it on her food-covered pants. "Here's my card with my contact information." She turned another card over to write on the blank side. "I'll need your number, so I can contact you."

Circles of hazel with gold flecks surrounded a pair of large dark pupils gazing down at her. Her knees wobbled. *It couldn't be. Could it? Not after all these years. Please, God, don't let it be him. Not now..* He reminded her of someone she once knew years ago, or at least thought she knew, before he ditched her.

The guy accepted her business card and handed her his. "Call me when you get it worked out. Keep the hundred as a deposit." He turned to leave when Abigail gazed at the name on the card. A name and number gilded in gold. *Phillip J. Barnes.*

She took a second glance at him. Tall, medium build. Deep, penetrating eyes. *Pip.* It was Pip. Abby locked her knees, so they wouldn't buckle, but remained calm outwardly. She must be wrong. This wouldn't be Pip. She shook her head. No. She must have hallucinated.

After swiping the smudged card on his pants, the familiar-looking person held it inches from his face to take a second look. *Abigail Harris Fitzgerald.*

"Abby? My Abby?" His countenance turned into a question mark.

"Pip?" Abby murmured. Her knees shook visibly, but, thankfully, he stared only at her face. Phillip Barnes, Pip, the boy she'd had a crush on ever since the day he walked into her fifth-grade class. The boy she hadn't seen in over forty years. A vision filtered through her remembrance: the hayride, the music streaming from the jam box, Pip's arms wrapped around her–.

"Abby?" Pip looked at her with the same quirky grin he had years ago. The same grin, which made her knees go all rickety-wonky, just as now.

The tic in Abby's left cheek twitched double time. He was saying something about lunch. She stared at him, not answering. Barely hearing much at all.

"So then, lunch tomorrow? We can crunch the figures together. I suppose you still live around here, huh?"

She willed her voice calm. "I moved away for a while but came back. What about you? I haven't seen you around." *Especially forty-some years ago when I needed you the most.*

"I'm visiting my niece, Janine, for a few days. She needed a dog sitter while she was on vacation. So, are we on for tomorrow? Noon all right?"

He was asking her to lunch after nearly biting her head off earlier. Or was it she who did the biting? Probably not a good idea. Best to refuse. She'd rather forget about him. "That's such a short time; I can't possibly finish the calculations."

"I'll help you after we eat."

Definitely not a good idea. Pip Barnes was a part of her life bygone. She didn't know this Phillip J. Barnes, and she surely didn't want him to know her. She might not identify with this stranger, but she could never forget Pip, no matter what name he used. Only the good Lord knew how hard she'd tried.

"Well, okay. We can meet here." Did she really just say she'd meet him? What happened to the not a good idea? Sometimes Abby couldn't trust her own mouth not to blurt out words best kept silent.

"Good. I'll look forward to it." He glanced up at the sign above the café and furrowed his brow again. "MsFitz?"

"That would be me, Ms. Abigail Fitzgerald." She grinned. "Some people around here think the other spelling a suitable name."

"I'm so glad I ran into you, Ms. Abigail Fitzgerald, but you don't look like a misfit to me." That grin again. Wobbly knees again. Then came the rest of the memory. Again.

A waitress, overhearing the conversation piped up. "Oh, that's not Miss Abby. People around here call us workers, Abby's misfits because–"

"Harper, Mr. Barnes doesn't want to hear all that." Abby waved her youngest worker to silence.

Phillip Barnes grinned at Harper. "You'll have to continue that story one day when she's not around. I'd love to hear it." He eyed Abby's food-covered face and clothing, without comment, took her sticky hand and said, "Until tomorrow then, Abby. I'm sorry I acted like such a heel."

"Not the first time," she said too low for him to hear, unless he read lips.

"We'll work it out. I promise." Evidently, he didn't read lips. She'd already committed herself to the luncheon. Might as well make the most of it.

"See you tomorrow noon. No, we had better make it around two after the lunch crowd thins, so we can hear ourselves talk. And don't worry; I won't try to swindle you, although, I sure need that money." She couldn't help the sly dig of sarcasm.

*****

Phillip hummed as he and Raney jogged back to his truck. He opened the door to let the dog in the front seat. "Well, old boy, you sure got me in a fine mess. The Abby I knew wouldn't try to rip me off, yet people can change in so many years. To this, I can attest." He frowned at his frayed knees and faced Raney. "She probably thinks I buy my clothes from the Outreach and will feel sorry for me."

When he returned home, Phillip went straight to his laptop and Googled his old chum: Abigail Harris Fitzgerald, retired teacher, now café owner, and author of one cookbook, several articles, and anthologies. A widow who lost her husband back in Nam. She probably didn't have a lot of money, but she shouldn't be in need—not enough to be sue-happy. No criminal records. Phillip closed his laptop.

He had actually Googled Abby. He should kick himself. She'd been his best friend for so many years and later, the love of his life. Abby was still pretty as ever. Black and gray droopy curls and chocolate smudged age lines didn't change Abigail. However, yesterday's Abby wasn't the contentious woman he'd met today. Whatever had happened to make Abby so angry? She had a right to be bitter toward him, he supposed. Yet she'd called him Pip. No one had called him Pip in the last forty-some years. He laughed inwardly.

Phillip's mind raced backward at an unstoppable speed to the early sixties when he first became good friends with twelve-year-old Abby. If a kid at thirteen can be in love, he had loved Abigail Harris. That was middle school. She liked him, too, but he wasn't sure how much. Then they entered high school. Her hair short with black curls framed her movie star face, her figure no longer that of his fishing pal, the tomboy kid. Abby was a cheerleader. He was just a country redneck. But she still cared for him, and that gave Pip more excitement than a free pass to Woodstock.

Alas, it was time to stop dreaming about Abby and get this business finished. Maybe they could be friends again. He'd relish reviving an old rapport. After negotiations and a signed, paid-in-full receipt, he'd tell her he wasn't the pauper he appeared to be, but a wealthy executive.

Noon the next day, Phillip studied his closet. He wanted to look nice when he met Abby for lunch. The way he dressed yesterday, in Janine's ex's old clothes, she must think him a bum. He chuckled to himself. He hadn't intended to get out of the truck, but his niece had interrupted him washing his car to drive her to work. Raney bounded out when he reached to close the door his niece, left open. The big mutt smelled food.

Phillip took his tailored suit from the closet and laid it across the foot of the bed while he searched for a suitable tie. Abby Harris had promised to meet him for lunch this afternoon. He wrinkled his brow. Would Abby have chosen to meet with him had she not had money to recoup? "Stop it, Phillip," he told himself. Not every woman's eyes held dollar signs. Not every woman was his ex-wife.

Had someone hurt Abby as Miriam had hurt him? Is that why she showed so much bitterness and anger? Anger caused many people to do things contrary to their nature. Wonder how much payment she expected from him. Not that he couldn't afford it, but he learned early on to never let anyone take advantage.

He returned his suit to its place in Janine's closet. No need to dress up merely to eat lunch in a little café. Still he wanted to look decent and he'd sent all his casual clothes to the laundry since he'd planned to go home tomorrow. Phillip pulled out a western style shirt and a pair of faded jeans Tom had left in the back of the closet. Phillip took a second look. He didn't blame Tom for leaving these behind.

Phillip thought about the Abby from his youth, and a prickly delight ran through him like back when he was a kid just entering puberty. He'd tingled from his head to his feet if she accidentally touched his hand. He once loved this girl. Had he ever truly stopped? He shook his head, telling himself not to revive those days. She could be remarried since the Google information was uploaded. Probably was by now.

Phillip wrote a mental note to go shopping tomorrow. It would be no problem now the dry goods store had moved back to Buckman Street. He didn't need

suits and ties for the little town of Shepherdsville, Kentucky. He planned to stay here a few days more than he'd anticipated
and needed more casual clothing. Janine might need her uncle around for moral support, and he might need to be here for
any reason he could invent. Losing contact with Abby again was not Phillip's plan.

*****

Abby rooted through her cedar-lined closet. She should have come up to her apartment earlier instead of waiting until the lunch crowd thinned. She gnawed on her bottom lip for a full minute. What in the world would she wear? She pulled on her charcoal hound tooth slacks and her pale gray, long sleeved, silk blouse and twisted in front of the mirror to assure the back fit perfectly. She slipped on the matching nipped-waist jacket with notched lapels. Fully dressed, she pivoted and stared at her reflection in the mirror. "What do you think?" she asked the image.

Exquisite. Expensive. Didn't you just say your finances were low?

Abby made a face and shrugged at her look-a-like. "They are now. Just blew a bundle on this suit. Perhaps I should take it back, since I don't have enough books left to do any signings. Lord knows how long before I get more printed."

The image grimaced. *Well, I hope you saved enough
to pay for your lunch. From the way he looked, Phillip Barnes may expect you to pick up the lunch tab. And after*

MsFitZ CAFE

what he did to you, you shouldn't care what he thinks about how you look.

"I'm only having lunch with him to get the money he owes me. Then he can go his way, and I'll go mine." She frowned. "What tab, it's my café?"

The image lowered her eyes and twisted her mouth in a facetious way, indicating she was about to say something Abby might not want to hear. *Seriously, Abigail, I admire the way you give of yourself to help those young women, but you deserve something for yourself, like something decent to wear.*

"I just bought this suit, didn't I?" Should she return it?

You know what I mean. You pay those servers more than you pay yourself. And maybe if you hired some experienced workers, the café would generate more profit.

Abigail shouldn't listen to that other self. "My girls depend on the good wages. I pay them to keep off welfare. They work hard and deserve an honest wage. I have enough saved to live on." Abby turned and pointed her finger at the mirror. "You know why I do this, and God willing, I'll continue doing it."

Did you tell him? You should, you know.

"Of course not. He has no right to know. Now crawl back in that mirror and hide your ugly face." She turned her back to the mirror but glanced over her shoulder.

And it wouldn't hurt if you lost some of that butt.

Abby wiggled her rear at the twin in the mirror, turned to her closet and took off her one and only Ann

Taylor outfit. Why would she want to impress Phillip J. Barnes, anyway? She didn't know the man anymore, and they were only meeting at her cafe, not the Varanese. He probably couldn't afford a glass of water and a toothpick at a place like that.

    The clock on her dresser read 12:45. Better get a move on. Abby stood in front of the closet, half-dressed, holding an empty clothes hanger. She placed the business suit back in the closet and removed a brown skirt and a peach sweater. She didn't need to put on airs for Pip Barnes, even if she'd always liked the way he'd said, "Ah-be." He said many other things several years ago. Things she'd like to forget—one night in particular down by the edge of the river right after the hayride. The night The Temptations crooned from the jam box. *"You're My Everything.* "The night she went sliding and tumbling down a rainbow toward the pot of gold, which turned out to be a kettle of shame. The next day Pip vanished from Bullitt County without even a goodbye. Oh well, that was then. She lived in the present now. Philip J. Barnes acted as if he didn't remember or care. So, would she. It was time to meet him for lunch and make a settlement.

    Since she lived in the apartment over the café, Abby got to the diner before Phillip arrived and took a booth in the back section. Harper breezed back with two glasses of water and menus. "Miss Abby's got a boyfriend. Miss Abby's got a boyfriend."

    "And Harper doesn't have a job. Harper just got fired," Abby prattled back at her. "Don't you have something to do in the kitchen? Aracella looks like she needs help." Abby whacked the young girl on the backside with a menu. "Go. Now."

    He probably had a wife, too.

MsFitZ CAFE

The bell over the door jingled and Phillip strode toward Abby. "It's good to see you, Abigail. For a while this morning, I thought I might have dreamt I found you again."

Abby tried not to sound bitter, but her words pierced even her ears. "Found me? I was never lost. If I remember correctly, you're the one who moved away without a word of farewell; never even called or wrote." Her voice almost broke, but she steadied it.

His face paled, his lips turned a shade lighter. "I'm sorry. One day I'll tell you all about it. I promise. For now, please believe I couldn't help it. My mom moved and forced me to move with her. I wasn't allowed to contact you."

This wasn't the time or place to argue. Let him think she believed that if he so wanted. She'd heard many excuses in her lifetime, but this one took more than the cake. It took the whole bakery. She forced a smile and suggested they get on with settling the agreement.

"Shall we eat before that itemized list of yours leaves a bitter taste in my mouth?"

The well-remembered grin softened his face, but not Abby. Did he really think she padded the estimate? Or was he being sarcastic? Either way, it wasn't funny. Not to her.

"Please. Let's not start the quibbling again. I don't have a completed list--just a few figures jotted down. You said you would help me with the final count. Remember?" She should have known better than to believe him.

Phillip splayed his hands in front of him, palms up. "Only joking. Promise. Don't want to fight with you, Abby."

"Neither do I, Phillip. Guess I had better get used to the name Phillip, since PIP makes me think you should wear a straw hat and chew on a twig to go along with the jeans. The idea of Pip in jeans and a straw hat turned back the clock for Abby. Mr. Barnes' old Alice Chambers tractor chugged noisily across the fields and around fences. Pip was on his way to see her. Oh he pretended he only wanted to go fishing in the blue gill hole or swimming in the creek, but Abby knew, and she was glad

Abby forced herself back to the present. I'm sure your wife calls you Phillip." Well that was obvious. She might as well have come out and said, "Are you married?" Not as if she cared.

"Yes, Miriam called me Phillip, but she divorced me years ago." He picked up her hand. "PIP sounds fine to me."

"I'm sorry." She pulled back her hand. He surely wouldn't be sweet-talking her to avoid liability for the damages. She wouldn't care for herself, but her young moms needed this money. Besides, he didn't have the right.

"I'm hungry. I can calculate better on a full stomach. What's good?" He scanned the menu.

Harper appeared from nowhere. "Chicken and dumplings. Everybody says Ms. Abigail Fitzgerald makes the best dumplings south of the Mason Dixon, and she came in at dawn to make them special for you. Cook didn't lay a hand on these babies. Not on Miss Abby's secret recipe."

Abby pretended to rub something out of her eye to hide the blush warming her cheeks. "Harper. I make dumplings every Wednesday. Today is no exception. Will you please take our order?"

They both ordered the dumplings, salad, and sweet tea. While waiting for the food, Abby folded and unfolded her hands as if she didn't know what to do with them. She picked up a fork. Laid it back down. Fidgeted with the napkin and placed it in her lap. Finally, she shoved the water glass aside and took a pen, paper, and calculator from her bag.

"Abby, put them away until we eat. Okay?" He brushed her hand as he reached for the water. She tingled as she did as a preteen and they went fishing or swimming in the river, not to mention the later emotions of a seventeen-year-old.

He continued as if nothing bothered him. "I need to tell you something about myself. I'm not what--"

A scream emanated from the kitchen. Abby and Phillip jumped from their seats and raced to see what was wrong. Aracella, the cook, lay prone on the floor while Harper stood over her holding a butcher knife.

Chapter Two

Phillip knelt beside Abby as she placed her fingers on Aracella's wrist feeling for a pulse. A sunray filtered through the window, glinted on the steel blade of the knife, and flashed across the room. Abby gasped. Her eyes bore into Harper. "What in heaven's name is wrong in here? Harper, what are you doing with that knife?"

The cook lay sprawled behind the counter. Sprigs of long, jet black sprouted from under the hairnet. She opened her dark eyes, looked up into three glaring faces, stared at the screen of the iPhone clenched in her hand, and closed them again.

Harper's face, two shades lighter than its normal caramel, looked at her employer. "Honest, I didn't do anything. Heard Aracella scream and ran to her. I was chopping vegetables. Don't know what happened. She just fell like a chunk of wood." Harper replaced the knife on the worktable.

"Would this have something to do with it?" Phillip pried a cell phone from Aracella's fingers. The screen held a copy of an ultrasound–a fetus curled up in its mother's womb.

Abby put a cold, damp cloth on Aracella's forehead. The cook opened her eyes and whispered, "Isabella."

"Isabella is your daughter, isn't she?" Harper asked.

"My precious Isabella." She made the sign of the cross. "Mary, Mother of God. Who has done this to my little girl?"

"What—" Harper's eyes widened.

Abby tapped Harper's shoulder. "Shhh, she's praying."

Phillip waited for Aracella to finish her Hail Marys and helped her stand. "Are you alright, ma'am?" Harper answered for her. "Of course, she is. Aracella can faint as easy as Chloe can butter her biscuits."

The cook wept around her words. "My baby. She's away at college. I only wanted a better life for her, but I sent her off to the city-- a den of immorality. Now she's with child." She scrutinized the baby boy image in the ultrasound.

The phone whistled. Aracella opened the next message. *So sorry. Sent message by mistake. My friend Demi's baby. Isn't he precious?*

Aracella dropped the phone as if it were on fire and swayed. Abby snatched the wet cloth and Phillip took hold of Aracella before she passed out again.

Aracella tilted her head slightly and half smiled. "It might have been nice to be a grandmamma."

Phillip escorted Abby back to their seat. What did he think of her misfits now? They might be oddballs, but they were her girls.

Madison the oldest of the waitresses came to their booth. "Looks like you had some excitement in here while I was at the bank."

"Yes, please bring me and my guest a fresh salad and another warm dish of the chicken and dumplings before you get bogged down in kitchen drama. We're starving. Madison meet my friend Phillip."

Phillip extended his hand.

Madison returned the handshake and. "I saw you yesterday, I believe. How is your friend Raney?"

Abby gave her waitress a stare and a nod that said, "Enough. Get us hot food." Madison returned to the kitchen, the cold lunch in her hands.

After Madison delivered the second lunch, Phillip smacked his lips. "I haven't tasted dumplings like this since I last ate at your mom's. Wow, home-cooked food. I'll bet your family loves these."

"Thank you but look around. These girls are my family." Abby lifted the papers from her briefcase. "We really must get down to this. I must help the girls clean up in here. Chloe is off today, so I need to pick up the slack." Was he trying to find out if she had a family? Hmm.

"Okay, if we must, but I dare say I enjoyed the floor show." Phillip grinned. "Just give me the figures you've worked up. I'll okay them."

"No, that wouldn't be fair. You take these with you and look them over. If they're more than you can afford, I'll recalculate." She shrugged. "Only estimates. I thought we would work on them together."

"Not necessary. I'll look them over and send you a check or better yet, drop it by tomorrow." He took the estimates and reached for her hand. "Abby, I do need to tell you something about myself. The clothes I wear are-"

"Pip, you don't have to explain anything to me. I don't care about money and clothes." She glanced at his faded jeans. "They hold no weight with me. Friends know no financial levels."

"Abby, please let me finish."

"Not another word. I have to help the girls." She left the papers with Phillip and disappeared into the kitchen.

"But I need to tell you…" She was already gone.

Now, old boy what do you do next? Phillip had tried to tell Abby who he really was, but she wouldn't listen. Truth was, he didn't try extremely hard. After reconnecting with Abby, he didn't want to do anything to lose her. He'd loved her back then. Now he was sure he'd never stopped

*****

Biscuit dough squished between Abby's fingers as she glanced at the clock over the opening behind the counter. She could set her watch by Madison reporting to work each morning at 5:00 a.m., because Madison was never late. Yet it was 5:50 and no Madison. Abby's left cheek twitched as a worry line creased her forehead. She relaxed at the sound of a key in the lock of the back door. Madison entered.

Each morning Abby made biscuits while Madison prepared the gravy for the breakfast crowd.

Abby glanced over her shoulder. "Madison, what's with the long face? You look so down in the dumps; it would take a backhoe to dig you out."

"What's not wrong? My washing machine broke last week. No sooner got it fixed 'til my septic tank backed up."

"Know of a good septic service?" She picked up the telephone book.

"Uhm, let me see. Yeah, I believe I do. Bullitt Septic Service. Jim Reading used to run the place. He comes in here all the time for biscuits and gravy. Seems like a nice guy. I think he retired, and his sons took over the business."

She laughed. "Tell them if they don't treat you right, Abby will stop the biscuits and gravy."

"That's what I like about Shepherdsville. Madison closed the phone book. "You don't need yellow pages here. Just ask Abby."

"Not all the time." She pointed a dough-covered finger. "Better get that gravy going. The Reading clan may be here for breakfast before you find their number."

Madison put down the book and started the gravy. She stirred the flour, bacon grease, and sausage mixture with a fury, daring it to lump. "Sorry, I didn't mean to complain. It's not just the money. The kids give me fits, and Simon only adds to the conflict with his condemnatory attitude. And of course, Noah hangs onto every word his daddy says. He's already beginning to act just like him, chauvinism, racism, and bigotry. Sometimes my son stretches my patience like a rubber band ready to snap."

Abby placed the biscuits into pans at just the right position, barely touching each other leaving room to expand with the heat. "Guess you do have a problem there. I can't see a child of yours with a prejudiced thought in his soul."

"And he wouldn't have if I had my say. On the other hand, Julianne thinks everything is acceptable. If you are an underdog, you are a hero in her book. It's hard to be a single mom, but harder to be a single mom with an ex-husband who contradicts every moral lesson I attempt to teach." She emptied the gravy into a steam table pan and gave a half grin. "Bet you didn't know I would dump all this on you when you inquired about my problems. Didn't mean to flood you with my troubles."

Abby placed two large pans of biscuits in the hot oven. "I wouldn't have asked if I didn't want you to answer. Besides, I got big shoulders." She patted herself above her upper arm. "Well-padded and soft too. Lean on them anytime you feel the need."

Abby put her hand in her apron pocket and fiddled with her ink pen. "I haven't scheduled you for a full workweek because I know how hard it is to keep up with your college classes and put in forty hours. If you need more hours, let me know." Abby had no idea how the restaurant would support more hours for anyone. She didn't pay herself minimum wage as it was.

The kitchen door swung open again. Chloe jogged into the café, chewing her gum faster than Dale Earnhardt, Jr. could race around the Daytona Speedway. She grabbed her apron. "Butter my biscuits, am I late?"

"No. you just made it again by a slim margin." Abby answered. "The crowd's has not knock the door down yet but go and open it before they do."

Abby put the last pan of biscuits in the oven. "Hold on, Chloe." She glanced at the clock and waved. "Wait a minute; we still have a couple of minutes before 6:30. Been wanting to talk to you about something." She motioned for Chloe to sit with her in the first booth.

"What's up, Miss Abby? Have I done something wrong?"

"No, sweetie, you haven't done anything wrong. You're one of the hardest workers I've ever had." Abigail squeezed her hand. "You're always here in time to serve breakfast. We're okay there."

"Then what...."

"Honey, it's your choice of clothing, and sometimes you flirt with the gentlemen customers. Now, mind you, you're trying to get your son back out of the system. What people think about you goes a long way. You're aware most of the social service caseworkers come here to eat. Especially when they're in court right across the street. The County Attorney. Judges, too."

Chloe twined her fingers one around the other. Her eyelids dropped so her eyes didn't meet Abby's. "You think I'm going back to my old ways; don't you? I'm not. I just play around with them. Heck, none of those men would give me the time of day, if we met on the street. They're judges and lawyers and such."

"Precisely. Just as I said." Abby hoped Chloe understood what she was trying to tell her. "I never doubted you. Just don't want anybody else to." She stood and looked at the clock. "It's time to unlock that door now. We'll continue this later." She put her hand on Chloe's shoulder. "If you ever need to talk, I'm here for you. I care about you, girl. Hope you know that."

"I do, Miss Abby, but butter my biscuits, I gotta be myself. I can't pretend to be somebody I'm not. Those men know I'm joking. They like it when I flirt with them. And that Mr. Tom Givhan, - he's a trip. Jokes right back as if he means it. I know he's jesting just like he knows I am. I'll get Wally back. You watch and see. I'm his mother." She walked toward the door, her short skirt hugged snugly under hips, and swayed in rhythm to her blonde ponytail sprouting from a big pink scrunchie on the top of her head.

"I hope you do. I hope you do." Abby watched Chloe, tongue in cheek. Next time she'd mention the length of that skirt. Maybe next time, Chloe would confide in her why they took her child away, but Abby didn't ask.

Chapter Three

Returning from the Post Office, Abby stopped on the sidewalk and chatted with a few customers, the last of the lunch crowd, before she entered the café. Harper met her by the register. "Miss Abby, you done gone and missed your sweetie. The sexy hunk came and left while you were at the Post Office."

"Phillip Barnes is not my sweetie."

Harper raised one of her eyebrows. "Then how come you knew who I was talking about. I could have meant Mr. Johnson or Mr. Pet--"

"Enough, Harper. What did he want?" That girl got 0n her last nerve at times.

"Mr. Barnes said tell you to take this check and he hoped it would help with the Mommy Fund. You know, Miss Abby, that's a good name for that charity of yours. Mommy Fund."

"I don't know about that. What else did he say?"

"He said he'd be back in a couple of days, but he had some business he needed to take care of in Chicago and was sorry he missed you."

"Well, if he thinks he's going to drop off a piddly little check for a few dollars, then weasel his way out of paying for what that dog did to my stuff, he'd better start thinking in another direction. He's good at pulling a disappearing act when it gets down to the nitty-gritty." Abby snatched the envelope from Harper. "This time it's not going to work."

She ripped open the envelope and staggered backward, balancing herself against the back of the booth.

"What is it Miss Abby?" Harper peeped over Abby's shoulder at the check.

"Is Aracella still here? I need her to come in here and faint for me."

"Well she can do that as easy as my phone can drop a call. But why? How much did he give you? Five hundred dollars?"

"No…"

"Didn't think so. Let me see." Harper looked over Abby's shoulder then yelled into the kitchen, "Aracella! Come in here and faint for both of us!"

Aracella and Chloe came running out. Harper waved the check she'd taken from Abby's hand. "Twenty-thousand, dollars. Mr. Barnes contributed twenty-thousand-dollars to the Mommy Fund."

Abby grabbed the check away from Harper and slumped down into the beige, leather-covered booth. She held it with the tips of two fingers like it might detonate. "What am I supposed to do with this? Where did Phillip get this much money?" Perhaps she'd layered it on a little too thick with the sob story about children and Christmas. He probably cashed in his life insurance policy or something. She hoped not.

"I think he can afford it, Miss Abby. Take another look." Chloe pointed to the signature, Phillip J. Barnes, from the account of Barnes & Barrett Publishing, Inc. Abby didn't think she needed Aracella to pass out for her. She could do it all on her own. Barnes & Barrett was one of the largest publishing companies in the country. She knew because she did her research before, she submitted the manuscript for her cookbook.

For once in her life, Abigail Harris Fitzgerald was speechless. She couldn't say another word. She quickly dropped into the first booth and stared at the check. Of course, she'd return it when and if he came back. He was probably living up to his old habits of leaving and not returning. Probably felt guilty for disappearing all those years ago. For all she cared, he could stay in Chicago and she'd mail it to him. Phillip Barnes didn't owe her anything.

Maybe he did owe her, but nothing he knew about. And nothing she was about to tell.

Abby continued to stew for the next few days. He'd actually let her believe he was poor. Didn't he trust her not to wangle money from him? Is that why he lied? Well, maybe lie was a bit strong, but in a sense, he lied when he omitted the truth. Just went to prove, if a person isn't trustworthy himself, then he tends to think the same about others. Phillip Barnes verified his unreliability many years ago. She couldn't believe how close she came to falling for his smooth words again, but this time she was not the same naïve young girl with a head full of dreams. She would not succumb to his magic— with or without the aid of The Temptations. Not even Lena Horne.

He probably didn't even remember that hayride back in that autumn when she was seventeen. Country kids had no trouble finding something to occupy their time in the crisp cool evenings of early fall. As he often did, the older brother of one of the teens hooked his straw-laden wagon behind a tractor and pulled the neighborhood gang through the back roads on a hayride. By the time they reached the big curve near Bernheim

MsFitZ CAFE

Forrest, the radio boomed. As Percy Sledge tingled her skin with "When a Man Loves a Woman," Abby's heart palpitated.
Couples paired off, Bob and Sue, Jim and Lou. Abby and Pip. They stopped by the creek at Bo Bilbray's farm where they made a fire ring and roasted hot dogs and marshmallows until it
was time to head home. She and Pip hopped off when they reached his car they'd left at Abby's dirt road.
Pip seemed so sad as he squeezed her hand and suggested taking a hike down by the river's edge before they drove home. She squeezed back and agreed to walk with him. Pip grabbed the jam box, took a quilt from his backpack, spread it on the riverbank, and turned on the music. They sat on the cover and stared up at the stars, munching on potato chips and grape sodas.
The stars twinkled like fireflies playing hopscotch through the Milky Way. "Look, there's the big dipper. And the little one," Abby pointed to the sky.
Pip took her hand. "The Milky Way. Hope it's the way into your heart. I couldn't stand life without you." He spoke with the voice of a scared little boy. Pip might not remember, but she'd remember that Friday evening for the rest of her life.
While Abby contemplated the meet-up with Phillip again, he walked into the café. She didn't say anything. Actions spoke louder.
"Hello, Abby. Sorry I missed you earlier."
"Yeah, me, too." She walked back to the coatroom, took the check from her purse, and placed it in his hand. "I can't accept this."
He raised one eyebrow. "Why not? I asked you to give me a figure. If it isn't enough, how much do you want?"

"I don't want anything from you, Phillip. Nothing at all. The Mommy Fund can survive without you. I'll find the money somewhere else." She squared her shoulders and turned to walk into the kitchen, the tic in her left cheek going into a spasm.

Phillip grasped her arm. "Wait. I tried to tell you who I am. Twice. You stopped me both times."

Abby's heart pounded. Her cheeks gave off heat. "You didn't try hard enough. I suppose you tried to tell me you were leaving Bullitt County, but I wouldn't let you. You tried to say you were dumping me, but I refused to listen? Strange, I don't remember any of that Pip. Oh, excuse me." She batted her eyes and lifted her voice. "I meant to say, Mr. Phillip J. Barnes."

He tightened his grip on her arm. "Come on, we're getting out of here. I need to talk to you. We have a lot of catching up to do."

She jerked her arm loose. "I have work to finish. Some of us little peons have to work for a living."

"Abigail, you are not being fair."

"Fair? I'll tell you what's not fair." She gained control before she said more than she wanted her girls to hear. "Okay. Let's go. My apartment's around back. Come let us talk." She held her head high and strutted to the stairs behind the café.

Phillip followed through the door of the second story apartment. "This is nice, Abby."

"Suits me. Nothing fancy like I'm sure you're accustomed to." Her eyes roamed over the comfortable sofa and over-stuffed chair. Cream-colored drapes complimented the background of the old rose and burgundy floral print. Nothing fancy at all, but it was hers.

Phillip didn't answer.

"Have a seat. I need some coffee." Hospitality was the furthest thing from her mind, but Abby needed a minute to compose herself. She wasn't sure why she was so angry Phillip had not told her he was rich.

"That would be good." He sat in the chair where she motioned him. "I'll take mine black."

She poured French vanilla creamer in hers and brought two cups to the living room coffee table. "Okay, Phillip, what is so important you want to tell me?"

He dropped his chin, his eyes lowered toward the toes of his John Lobb shoes. "Abby." He lifted his eyes to meet hers. She could almost believe she saw something deep and sincere in them. She looked away, before she began falling for his lies again.

Phillip linked fingers of both hands. "I am sorry. I can't tell you everything even now, but I had no choice other than to leave the state. My mother went into a witness protection program and we lived incognito until Dad was arrested and convicted."

"Oh." What else could she say except add, "I didn't know. Didn't hear anything on the news."

"No one did. Authorities kept it quiet to protect Mom and me."

Abby studied his eyes, brown mingled with gold like gold dust in the sand. Could she believe him? He certainly had no reason to make up a story just to impress her. "But I never heard from you again. Not until the bake sale."

"I tried, Abby. I tried. I came back and questioned all our classmates. No one knew where you were. Finally, your mother told me you had gotten married. You didn't sit home and worry about me before the school year ended."

"She just told you that. It was years after you left me before I married. I did finish school. Just not in Bullitt County. I-I thought you didn't care." Should she open a window? It was difficult to breathe when her heart played hopscotch on her rib cage. What should she say? She didn't want to tell him. Not yet. Some things worked out better left unsaid.

A hint of a tear glinted in Phillip's eye. "I thought what we had was deep enough you'd have waited a while. At least until I found a way to contact you. You should have known I would. I was gone six months, a lifetime for me. I assumed you felt the same."

"How was I to know you couldn't contact me? I was heartbroken and humiliated. I'd never been with another boy.

Some days I thought you left because you didn't respect me anymore. Other times I could see that silly grin of yours like you had when you won that bass fishing trophy. You always reveled in a new conquest."

Phillip put the coffee cup on the end table, clutched her shoulders, and gently shook them. "Abby, Abby, I never. You knew I would never."

"I didn't know anything. Nothing except I gave myself to you and never saw you again. Do you know how dirty I feel even until this day?"

"You weren't dirty, and definitely you were not a conquest."

She shrugged. "I met Paul a few years after you left. He knew you had broken my heart, and he was so gentle and patient with me. And he loved me enough ..."

Her voice trailed off from an unfinished sentence. "We didn't have time for a long courtship before Paul shipped out. He was in the 101st Airborne of Ft. Campbell and going back to Vietnam. We only had two weeks after marrying before he left." The small twitch in her left cheek accelerated.

"I'm sorry, for your loss. I really am. I was in the Reserves. Was about to be called up for oversees duty when the war ended."

"It was good you didn't have to go."

"Guess I've always been lucky like that. The Army paid for my college, and I went on from there to create a new life for myself. Forgive me, Abby, but I must ask you. Did you love him?"

What was she supposed to say? How was she supposed to answer?

"Did you love him, Abby?" he repeated.

"Yes, but not in the same way I did you. You were my best friend and my first love. My first passion. Paul was there for me when I needed him, even though several years had passed, and I suppose you might say I was still on the rebound. A cliché, I know, but I can't think of another way to say it. Paul was good to me. He loved me very much. Of course, I loved him." She twisted the ring she still wore on her left finger. "What about you? You said you were married. Did you have children?"

"It didn't work out. And no, we never had children. We divorced after ten years of fighting."

"I'm sorry. Did you love her?"

"I don't know. I thought I did, but looking back, maybe I never did. You cast a light, which no woman could ever outshine. Did you have children?"

"Paul and I never had children. I preferred to wait until the war was over. The war was over for Paul during a twenty-three-day battle with the North Vietnamese Army. Four hundred and twenty-two American soldiers died. Paul was one of them." Her voice broke, but she nodded toward the mantle with his picture, certificates, and medals, a Purple Heart, and a Medal of Honor. "He drove a truck filled with ammunition through a burning village. He saved many of his buddies but lost his own life."

"I'm sorry." Phillip murmured. "I know I'll never live up to that, but, Abby, I love you." He brought his lips close to hers. His breath whispered across her face. Abby's lips parted for a split second before she pulled away.

The bitter grudge she'd carried for so many years lay heavy on her heart. She didn't know how to accept guilt when it landed in her own lap. Guilt for not trusting Phillip. Guilt for not being fair to Paul. Guilt for being selfish.

"Why didn't you wait for me, Abby?"

"Phillip, I don't know what to say. I can't give you an explanation now, except I was hurt. I was angry, bitter and most of all, violated." She should tell him everything, but she couldn't. She couldn't yet.

Phillip didn't press Abby. He took a drink of coffee. Abby sipped hers. Phillip looked out the window. Abby
wiped a drop of coffee from the table. Quiet thundered through the apartment.

Phillip arose and walked toward the door but stopped. "The check, Abby. I want you to keep it." He placed it on the table.

"No, you don't owe me anything." However, she owed him. She owed him the truth. She wanted to tell him right now and opened her mouth but froze. The buried words were too entrenched to come out.

Phillip continued. "It's not for you. I want to contribute to the mothers and young children. I have the money, and they need help. Please let me help make their life easier."

She didn't know what to do. She could hold a dozen benefits and never raise that much money before winter. Probably never. Her mind raced back to Madison and her two teenagers. It would lift a huge burden if they didn't have to worry when Simon was late with the next child-support check.

"Don't force them to suffer for what I did to you. If you refuse the money, I'll give it to another charity," Phillip said. He put up both palms, splayed his fingers as if fending her off. "I didn't mean that. Didn't mean you're a charity. Meant to say, I'll find a charity to donate it."

Phillip was almost pathetic with his effort not to offend her. She couldn't help herself. She laughed.

Now he was pathetic. The expression on his face said, "Should I smile or run for cover?"

"I'll take the check, Phillip. We are a charity. The kids will thank you and the mothers will fall in love with you." She tucked her guilt into the back of her mind and promised herself she'd explain everything when she knew this Phillip a little better.

Phillip left Abby's apartment. He really should go back to Chicago. Janine didn't need him so much now she'd found someone to walk Raney and grew more comfortable in her own skin since the divorce. Part of him said to leave and not pursue the past, but another part couldn't shake the feeling Abby wasn't telling him everything. To tell the truth, he wasn't ready to leave with a great divide still between them. Maybe he'd go to the family home in Prospect where his grandparents used to live. Far enough away from Shepherdsville, he could reason his emotional state without running into Abby every time he turned around. Yet, not so far, he couldn't come back in an hour or so if he chose.

The board members, his partner, and editors proved capable of running a publishing house and gave him opportunity to downsize his involvement in the company. His presence functioned more for his own benefit than for the advantage of the business. Phillip regarded himself as old when he thought of fully retiring. Yet, around Abby, the years slipped away. He became the kid driving a farm tractor cross-country to see his girl. Was it possible they had another chance in their sixties? He shrugged. Who ever said love had an age limit? Would she think him senseless if he asked her to go back to the farm with him to go fishing? Phillip grinned. He bet she could still slide a worm on a hook without a grimace. Abigail Harris Fitzgerald was one tough woman.

Chapter Four

Abby took off her blue-checked apron and hung it on the hook in the kitchen, glad it was closing time. Madison looked around and seeing no customers, whispered, "I met with another situation when I got home."

"What can I do?"

"Just let me cry on your shoulder like you always do, I guess. Miss Abby, I don't know what I'd do without you."

"Come, sit with me. It can't be all bad." She led Madison to the front booth and patted her own shoulder. "Put it here."

"As I said, I rushed home from school. Julianne didn't know I was coming. And there she was, sitting in the middle of her bed and Kyle sitting on the foot. She knows better. I think I'll quit school. Stop working and go on welfare. Just stay home and take care of my kids."

"Madison, what were they doing?"

"Homework."

Abby lifted her brow. "And they didn't know yowere coming home?"

"No. "

"And they were fully dressed?"

"Yes."

"No alcohol? No drugs?"

"Nothing I could see."

Madison peeked over her plastic frame glasses at Abby. "Abigail Fitzgerald, you can answer more questions by simply asking them than anyone I know." Madison gave her a thin grin. "You think I'm building a mountain out of mud pies, don't you? But I have rules, and I insist my children obey them."

"I understand, Madison."

"I know I'm old fashioned, but I can't change the way I am."

"Honey, it isn't for me to tell you what rules to render." Abby reached across the table and squeezed Madison's hand. "For what it's worth, I agree with you, but make sure Julianne knows you are upset because she disobeyed, not because you think she's bad."

"I don't think she's bad, but I expect her to respect and obey me."

"Then the two of you need to talk. Really talk." If only Abby's mother had talked with her.

"I'm going to do just that, right now. Thank you, Miss Abby."

Before Madison could leave, Julianne bounded through the back door. "Mom, it's important I talk to you, but first, I need to go to the ladies' room. I'll be right back."

She sounded so serious and sad; Abby worried what it was. Her mind sought the meaning of Julianne's words, as she was sure, so did Madison's. Did she want to move in with her dad because she was angry with her mom? No, she doubted that. According to Madison, Julianne would rather move into a convent than into the house with Simon and Lisa.

Madison spoke low to Abby, "My sixteen-year old can't be pregnant. Now I understood why Aracella fainted. Maybe she wants a car. Yes, probably so. But what if she's in love with Kyle and wants to get married? What if...? What did Julianne want to tell me?"

Julianne broke the whispers. "Mom, I'm sorry I disobeyed you."

"I'm sorry, too. You know my rules, Julianne. I was on my way home to discuss those rules with you, but I sense you have something deeper on your mind. We'll put the disobedience on the back burner, but know it is not forgotten." She walked around the table and stood behind Julianne. "Go ahead and tell me what's bothering you."

"Mom, I do need to talk, but I don't know how."

Madison stroked her daughter's long, blond, straight hair. "Honey, I usually find it best to just blurt it out. I'll listen. I promise."

Julianne's blue eyes looked up at her mother with such sincerity, they tugged at Abby's heart. "Mom, please don't judge him."

"Judge who?"

"Kyle."

What had these kids done? It looked serious. "Do you two want me to go upstairs for a few minutes?" Abby asked.

"No, Miss Abby, you can hear this. Maybe you won't be prejudiced."

Madison drew in a long breath. "Julianne, I don't have a clue what you're talking about, but I don't usually pass judgment. I try to give God that job."

Abby sat silently by while Julianne reached up and squeezed her mother's hand. "I know, Mom. The reason I invited Kyle into my room is—well, I don't think of him as a boyfriend. You know Kyle and I have been friends since middle school. We both moved to this section of Bullitt County about the same time and attend the same high school."

Thank God, she wasn't pregnant. Abby should leave them alone.

Madison answered, "Yes, I know, I always thought you liked him."

"I do, but not in that way."

"Okay, I understand, but why…"

"Kyle's being bullied Mom, and I'm scared for him."

Madison slowly slid into a chair beside Julianne and slipped an arm around her shoulders. This conversation was getting deep. "Come on, honey, just spit it out. Who's bullying him and why? And why are you afraid?"

"Mom, Kyle is—" Julianne stopped mid-sentence when the back door squeaked, and Noah poked his head around it.

"Noah, I thought you were at Bob's," Madison said.

"I was, but something came up. His parents had to leave, so they dropped me off here."

"Son, your sister was telling me something in confidence. Can we just go home to finish this?" She looked at Julianne.

"Don't matter. I already know. She's trying to tell you her boyfriend's gay. Now, what do you think of little miss perfect? I thought we were Christians."

MsFitZ CAFE

Abby thought Madison might pass out.
Julianne clenched her fists. "Noah, you have no right. It's bullies like you who scare me! It's because I'm a Christian that I have compassion."
"Is compassion accepting everything coming and going? *You* scare *me*!" He stood in front of his mom and sister.
Abby decided not to leave. Madison might need her.
"Mom, you gotta put a stop to Kyle coming to our house. He creeps me out when he looks at me."
"When did Kyle ever hit on you?" Julianne smirked at Noah.
Noah half laughed; half sneered. "Never. He knows better."
"And he won't. He has better taste. And, besides, I never heard of Kyle coming on to anyone, boy or girl." She answered the hatred in her brother's eyes.
"Stop it you two. I'll have no more name-calling. And no more religious insults. I'm ashamed of both of you.
'I can't believe my friend and employer is being forced to observe such lewd behavior."
Abby fanned her hand, showing Madison it was ok.
"Look. I'm going to say this one time. You have both been taught Christian values and are old enough to interpret them." A mother can only lead, not coerce her children to share her beliefs."
How in the world was Madison going to appease both her children? What would she do if it were she?

Then Abby reminded herself, it would never be her. She had no children to appease.

"But Mom—"

"You will have your turn, Noah. I expect you to show your sister and Abby some respect. We are leaving."

Noah gritted his teeth, then mumbled, "My sister doesn't deserve any respect."

"Okay, Noah, I've had enough." Madison stomped her foot. "You keep quiet and get in the car. If you had asked me to talk to you personally, I would do it. You're grounded for your sassy mouth until I get to the bottom of this." She turned to Abby. "I am so sorry."

"It's all right."

"Yes, ma'am." Noah went out the back exit. Abby was sure that ma'am wasn't a term of respect but of rebellion.

"What Noah said might be true, but so what?" Julianne said.

"Honey, are you sure? This could be problematic and sticky." Madison appeared close to speechless. "I'm trying to comprehend. Give me some time here to absorb this. Kyle has been in and out of our house for years and I never suspected. I thought he liked you. Do you know for a fact he's-- that way?"

"Just say the word, Mom. 'Gay.' No, I don't know for sure. Kyle knows he can tell me anything, and he will when he's ready. I'm sorry if I disappoint you and Noah, but he's my friend, and he will always be. Mom, I know how Dad, Noah, and our church feel about gay people. It's just I need my mom to understand me."

Sweetheart, just because we might not agree with their way of life, doesn't mean we hate them. We love everyone."

Julianne rubbed her fingers through her hair. "I'm scared for Kyle. The kids at school are treating him terrible."

Madison swiped her hand across her forehead. "I'm your mom and I trust you to form the right opinions. I'll never tell you to stop being friends with Kyle. However, I am also Noah's mom. I have to look at his side of this picture."

Abby wished Madison had a good, moral husband to help with the kids. She watched Madison wringing her hands until they were red. Her lips moved silently below closed eyes. Madison was whispering a prayer.

Julianne scrunched the corner of the tablecloth in her fist.

Madison answered Julianne, "I have to allow Noah to tell me his side before I make any decisions. Whether I condemn or condone Kyle's lifestyle isn't the argument here. I don't want my family torn apart."

"Mom. My friend needs me. Do you understand?"

Madison closed her eyes and lifted her head. "Yes, and I'll always be here for both of you kids. I won't choose your friends, but it's my duty to guide you. I wish the two of you would've confided in me before this situation got out of hand. I've not had time to swallow this news, much less digest it. You must realize Noah lives here, too. I must keep our home comfortable for both my children to live in."

"But Mom…"

"Julianne, I'm not saying you have to stop being friends with Kyle. I do ask you to give me some time to talk to Noah before I make a hasty decision. Need to pray over it, too. One thing I can promise you is there will be no bullying coming from this house."

Abby couldn't hold her tongue any longer. "Sorry to butt in here, but exactly how are they bullying him?"

"Kids are altering photos of Kyle's face onto a woman's body. I don't wish to describe the rest." Julianne sunk her head into her mom's bosom. "I don't know if Noah is in on that or not, but he sure doesn't disagree with it. He thinks it's funny. There are other kids who openly admit their sexuality difference, and they don't get bullied." The young girl pulled away from her mother and sat down, hugged her knees, and bit her lips. "I don't know how much more Kyle can take. I'm worried about him, Mom, I'm worried. Afraid he may run away–or worse."

Chapter Five

Chloe, in a bright red sweater, breezed in the back door as the first customer walked through the front one.
"Her skirt is actually a good inch longer than usual. Did you discuss a dress code with her?" Madison asked.
"Not in the manner you mean. I hinted she make a few changes for the sake of Wally. Maybe she listened. I hope she'll make changes in her life for herself, instead of me demanding a dress code. I believe she will. Chloe's a good person."
"Abby, you think everyone is a good person."
"I believe underneath, we all have good qualities. To bring them out, it takes love and understanding."
"Then maybe you need to understand Mr. Phillip a little more, so you can see what lies beneath his flaws–whatever they are. I haven't seen any of them yet."
"Well, I-I … Maybe I do at that, Madison." Abby grinned. "Maybe I do, and maybe I will if I ever see him again. What about Simon? Have you considered—?"

Madison interrupted her. "He's a lost soul not looking for redemption."

"I believe that might be true. But get on out of here if you want to make your class on time. Abby told Chloe she'd be working the floor with her today, took a handful of menus in one hand, a coffee carafe in the other, and made her way to the back tables where a group of ladies sat with their heads huddled together. She recognized them as clerks at the courthouse. "Good morning, ladies. What can I get you to drink?"

Abby knew one of them as Janie. Maybe… Could be. Same hair and hazel eye color, but her face -- could resemble her mother. She didn't look a thing like Phillip.

Abby poured Janie's coffee and smiled pleasantly. She responded with a twinkle in her eyes, "Miss Abby, I'm Janine. My uncle told me you were old school chums. It sure is good to see the sparkle in his eyes again."

Abby could keep the coffee hot merely by holding it near her face. "Phillip and I were friends back in school."

"Well, he's not my real uncle, but he's my dad, Joey's, cousin. Long story there."

"Joey! I know him back from when Phillip and I were kids. It was nice to run into your uncle again."

"From what I hear, it was Raney who ran into you. I am so sorry about that. Uncle Phillip said he made restitution. I hope you've forgiven us."

"It was an accident. No forgiveness necessary. It certainly is nice to learn you are Janine. I thought as much." She poured the coffee for the rest of the table.

*****

The next day, Chloe left early for a meeting with the Social Services, leaving Harper and the cook alone in the cafe. The bell over the front door chimed, announcing a late lunch visitor. Harper peeked around the door and yelled, "Be with you in a few."

"Take your time. I didn't come to eat. Just stopped in to see Abby." Phillip joined Harper behind the counter and poured himself a cup of coffee.

"She's not here. She's gone to the bank." Harper nudged him in the ribs. "You better get out from behind this counter before Miss Abby comes back and puts you to work."

"Yes, and she'd do it too. Guess I'd better pull my weight around here or she'll charge me for this coffee." He rolled up his sleeves and delved into the dishwater, wiping down appliances, catsup bottles, and counter tops.

"Well, where have you been hiding? I didn't know you could work like this?" Harper tied an apron around him.

"Where do you think I got my spending money while attending college?"

"Then you're a self-made man, huh?" She figured a man like him had come from a wealthy family. He stood a foot taller in Harper's eyes.

"I sure am. Abigail and I grew up together. Both on small farms. Neither of us had much money." Phillip's honey-gold hazel eyes twinkled at her. "So, what's your story, Harper? Abby aids young ladies with children, but where do you fit in such a category?"

"I been wondering myself, Mr. Barnes, but I was afraid to question her about it. Didn't want to poke a blind horse in the eye."

"You don't have any children, do you, Harper?"

"No. Don't think I ever want any."

"You're still young. How old? About eighteen?"

"I'm nineteen and old enough to know I don't want to be responsible for kids. I couldn't offer them any kind of life."

"Don't say that. You have a lot to give."

"What? I didn't even finish high school. I can't raise a family working in a cafe the rest of my life."

"Then do something about it. Get your GED. Go to college. You can do that."

"No, I can't, Mr. Barnes. I can't read and write much at all. I gave up trying in the tenth grade. Just couldn't do it. My aunt says I'll be working in a go nowhere job the rest of my life. Just like her. She cleans at the hotel."

Abigail Harris Fitzgerald swooped through the back door. "Harper! Do not ever let me hear you talk about
yourself like that again. If I do, you are fired. Do you hear me? Fired."

"Miss Abby, you know it's the truth. Aracella can hardly make out my tickets when I take the orders. I just can't write. Almost not at all."

"I know that Harper, but you have a brilliant mind. I've been waiting for you to trust me before I said anything. Now I think I have an idea."

"You know I trust you, but what good does that do?"

MsFitZ CAFE

"I'm going to pay for you a tutor from our Mommy Fund. I'll find somebody to help you read and write and get your GED. I've been keeping some of the notes you've written, and I let a good friend, special education teacher,
look at them. She thinks you have a learning disability which, with help, you can overcome."

"But Aunt said…"

"Your aunt may have been wrong. She wasn't trained to help you."

A good feeling ran from Harper's feet all the way up
to her head. "Really, Miss Abby? Do you mean that?"

"Of course, I mean that, and with your permission, I want to look around to find you the right tutor. Just give me a couple of days to piece it together."

"Miss Abby, you can do anything. I never saw a problem you couldn't fix."

A wave of sorrow flowed over Miss Abby's face. Something Harper had never seen before. "I can't fix everything sweetie. I wish I could."

Doubts crept back into Harper's mind. "Maybe one thing you haven't thought about is I don't drive. I never could read that manual enough to pass my drivers' test. Anyway, I don't have a car. How could I get to a tutor? My Aunt drops me off here on her way to work. You know I live back on Ridge Road. Some call it the boondocks. Others say I live in the Bottoms."

"That's all a part of this puzzle I'm working out in my head. Like I said, give me a few days."

"Miss Abby, you got me so stirred up, I won't be able to sleep for a week. Wait 'til I tell my aunt. Maybe if that tutor can fix me, then I can fix Aunt Nellie. She can't read any better than me."

"When you talk to your aunt, you might ask her if she'd mind if you spent a few nights with me each week. I need help keeping the apartment clean." She leaned over and massaged her right knee. "I'm not getting any younger and there are a lot of things I'd rather spend my time on than cleaning house. You could pay me for room and board by working a few hours a week."

"I don't know what she'll say to that, but I know I'll say YES, and I'm old enough to make up my own mind."

"And what did you say back there about me being a blind horse? Are you calling me a blind horse?"

"No ma'am, Miss Abby. That's just an old saying my gramps used to say when he couldn't figure out what was going on. I'd never call—"

Abby laughed at Harper's reaction and cut off her words. "Shhh, Harper. I know. I was only joking."

Harper turned the light palms of her brown hands upward. "Whew. You gave me a scare. I sure didn't mean to insult you. I gotta make up my mind to be more careful with Gramp's old sayings."

"Then make up your mind to get this kitchen cleaned up so we can get out of here." Abby picked up a towel and swatted Harper's rump.

"Yes, Ma'am." She grabbed her behind with both hands in pretend pain. "Why you always zapping at me?"

"Cause I love ya." Abby smiled.

Phillip took off his apron. "Harper, you don't mind finishing up by yourself, do you? I think I'll

MsFitZ CAFE

persuade Abby to go home and get all spruced up. I'm taking her out for dinner tonight."

"Harper spread her lips until delight filled half her face. "No, sir, I don't mind at all. You've already done all the hard work anyway. You take Miss Abby out and show her a good time. That lady deserves to be strutted around the town."

"Uhm, I think you two forgot something." Abby darted her eyes from the young lady to the older gentleman. "No one asked me."

Phillip copied Harper's grin. "I was getting around to asking after I paved the way with Harper, so you wouldn't have an excuse to say no."

Abby pulled a little notebook from her pocket, thumbed through the pages, and answered, "You're in luck. I happen to be free tonight."

Abby rushed up to her apartment where she fussed with her closet. Why did she not have anything appropriate to wear? She had one good outfit amidst a closet full of nothing. If she had time, she'd go shopping and buy herself something soft and feminine. She pursed her lips, winked at the image in her mirror6, and decided to do exactly that. Phillip wouldn't be picking her up for two hours. A quick shower and a handful of curly mousse was all she needed. She could get to that new Goody's store and back in an hour if she could walk in, pick out the perfect outfit, and leave. *Yeah. Maybe.*

Fortunately, Goody's wasn't crowded, and they had a good sale to boot. In less than thirty minutes, she came out with a flowing, navy blue skirt and a sheer blue and white floral blouse. The shoes, sweater, and purse already in her closet would match. The white pearls in her jewelry box would complement the neckline perfectly. Not too fancy, but nice enough.

When Phillip knocked at her door, she met him with pleasure lighting up her face.

"You look pretty, Abby. I love your outfit."

"Thank you. I came home and rested a bit. Since you didn't say where we were going, I didn't know how to dress. I hope this is appropriate." She smoothed the flared skirt.

"Abby, you're appropriate in anything you wear. You are a beautiful lady."

She amazed herself acting so coy and rested when in fact, she'd just finished with the last bit of make-up before his knock sounded at the door. Abby smoothed the curls with her fingers, glad she'd moussed her hair instead of taking the time to use the curling iron.

Phillip, handsome in his blue suit and blue and white tie looked as if he'd dressed to complement her. Abby
glanced through the open bedroom door at their reflection in the mirror. The lady in the mirror smirked, and Abby winked back at her. She and Pip made an attractive couple. Always had.

MsFitZ CAFE

Chapter Six

Abby caught her breath when Phillip turned the Lexus down Frankfort Avenue. Were they going where she hoped they were? Yes, Phillip pulled into the curb under the sign, "Varanese." Not quite as swanky as she'd imagined, but the easy-going atmosphere and light Jazz music wafted all around. Who needed swanky? She fell in love at first sight with this Varanese.

Phillip grasped her arm at her elbow. The twinkling candles put of a soft glow inside the restaurant. "Oh Phillip, I've wanted to eat here ever since I watched the first review on 'Secrets of Louisville Chefs.' I wanted to jump into the TV screen and join the excitement," Abby said. "That Chef John is cute as a button, but those inside waterfalls and the live jazz, well, they just called my name."

"I'm happy I chose it." Phillip smiled, and patted Abigail's hand tucked into the crook of his arm." I Googled for the most romantic restaurant in Louisville, and here we are. Louisville's best American cuisine."

They entered the sliding glass doors into the open front dining area. The unique timbre of water cascading over a twenty-foot slate wall formed awe-inspiring falls that reverberated a soothing, melancholy ambiance. They must have followed the maître d to the table, but Abby couldn't bet on how she got there. Perhaps her feet left the floor and floated to the rhythm of smooth jazz.

Abby made a mental note to beg, borrow, or steal the recipe for the fried green tomato salad. Philip ordered the stuffed grape leaves. "A gorgeous plate to fix your eyes on," Abby said. She needed something to begin the

conversation. Keep it light and impersonal. Commenting on the fabulous display of the food seemed a good starting point.
Phillip must have been on the same level. "Yeah, rice, beans and beef, too."
"Mandarin orange & baby greens garnish it rather nicely." She should say something other than discussing the food; yet what? Forty-years was a long time, but Phillip came to her rescue with an easy conversation to follow. They discussed Bullitt County and agreed on how it had changed. They discussed the school system and the changes made since he left the county several years before. Phillip, always an easy guy to converse with, helped Abby relax and stop worrying. A few times, she slipped back in time and talked with Pip, but she always came back to the present. However, this present promised a memory of its own, especially when the live jazz band, occupying one corner of the dining room, played an oldie from 1975, a rendition of Lena Horne's *Love Me or Leave Me*.

They finished the meal and promised the waiter they would be back for dessert another evening when they were not so stuffed.

Maybe next visit, it would rain, and she could see the green waterfall running from the open roof. Abby had a weakness for waterfalls. She'd promised herself to see Niagara Falls someday, but instead, she sank all her cash into the "Mommy Fund."

Phillip started a sentence with "Abigail...," and then fell silent.

"Yes, Pi-- Phillip?" She almost said Pip.

He reached across the table and took her hand. "I wish we were younger and had our life in front of us. I'd like to court you, take you to romantic restaurants, and show you Paris, but as you know, we're well past the age of teenage immortality. Our time cries out to be used wisely."

She'd never dreamed they would ever be together like this. Not now, at this age. She toyed with her white linen napkin, folding, and unfolding it. "Phillip, I—I don't know what to say. I prayed so hard to hear those words when we were young. I thought our time had passed." Was it too late now?

"We're not too old, Abby. We still have several good years left. Let's make the best of them – together." The gold flecks in Pip's hazel eyes glistened. His tone of voice tugged at her heart. "What do you say, Abby? Shall we?"

Abby's fork clattered to the floor. She quickly lowered her head as she leaned over to retrieve it, so Phillip wouldn't see the ghosts struggling behind her own eyes. She wasn't prepared for this. How could she tell him what she'd done to their child? He'd never understand and forgive her, just as she'd not completely forgiven him. If he'd been there for her, they'd have a daughter now and probably grandchildren. Laying the fork back on the table, she chose her words carefully. "I need time, Phillip. Too much has happened. Too many mistakes. Too much hurt."

Could things ever be right for Pip and her? Would there be a time when they could look back on the past and not feel pain? She thought not. The pain, the fear and the insecurity were as real as the love they once shared.

Phillip leaned forward and buried both her miniscule hands in his burly ones. "I want to make up for all the mistakes and heal the hurt. Please, Abby, won't you give me another chance? I love you. I always have. Look into my eyes and see into my heart."

Her eyes met his. "I think I'll always love you, Phillip, but you don't understand. I haven't told you everything."

"You don't need to tell me everything, Abby. Just tell me you love me."

She looked into his eyes and the years slipped away. Pip was here with her again. "I do love you, Pip. I never stopped."

He caressed each of her fingers with the tips of his and gently turned her palms up, brushing his lips across them. "Let's get out of here. You've made me the happiest man in the world. I want to kiss you."

"Phillip..."

He held her wrap and she snuggled into it. Phillip said she didn't have to tell him everything. At least for tonight, she wouldn't tell him anything. Especially until after she'd gotten the good night kiss, he'd promised. One kiss and she'd put her past behind her where it must remain.

During the quiet thirty-minute drive home, she laid her head on his shoulder as he found the jazz station on the Sirius Radio. This is where life should have led them. Did they, in their sixties, dare travel this path now?

Phillip pulled into her drive behind the MsFitz Café. She turned toward him. "Thank you, Phillip, I had a wonderful evening."

"Do you mind if I come up for a while? A cup of coffee would be good." His hand grasped the door handle.

An answer waited on Abby's tongue. "Chloe has an early appointment with her lawyer, so Harper is spending the night and working the breakfast shift tomorrow. I'd hate to wake her."

Abby was glad Harper was there. She didn't want to make the same mistake she'd made nearly a half century ago, and she could not guarantee she wouldn't. Her heartbeat wildly, and her nerve fibers tingled at the possibility of being alone with Pip again. She mentally shook herself and told the seventeen-year-old within to still, because she no longer existed. Perhaps Abby had subconsciously anticipated this when she invited Harper to stay over.

They reached the door of her apartment. "In that case, we'll say goodnight here." Phillip tilted Abby's chin with a finger and locked his gaze into hers. She trembled. He trembled. He pulled her close and their lips met, soft and gentle as young lovers. An imprisoned passion loosed, and they clung to each other. Abby almost regretted asking Harper to stay over. She pulled away. Pip and Abby again. Did she dare? This was exactly what she'd feared. Thank goodness, The Temptations weren't singing.

Aware of the sparks a few kisses could ignite, she'd be careful. After all, she and Phillip were Christian adults. Senior citizens even. They could enjoy each other's companionship without intense passion. She would walk a narrow path and see where it led. Maybe it could lead to forgiveness for them both. It was good to

have Pip back into her life. Why go and ruin it with a confession about something she could never change?
She tiptoed quietly into the apartment. Harper was in bed and hopefully, asleep. Abby wasn't up to Harper's interrogation on how the date had gone. It wasn't a date anyway. Just two old friends having dinner at a nice restaurant. At least that was all the information Abby was prepared to give.

Flames engulfed the gas log in the fireplace. A chill had fallen over all of Kentucky this early fall morning.
Abby's apartment was no exception. She dressed quickly before running downstairs to the café and made the biscuits. Madison could oversee the rest of the pre-breakfast preparations. She rushed back to the apartment and slipped into jeans and a sweater. She and Phillip had plans.
Aromas of fried chicken escaped from the packed basket. One of their favorite places in the world called out to Abby and Pip. Bernheim Forest once was their chosen place
to walk trails and have picnics. Today they'd celebrate those remembrances. She'd vowed not to let her emotions for Pip come alive again, but just a short time alone wouldn't hurt. She needed that much.

Abby couldn't remember the last time she visited Bernheim, but she remembered the hours she and Pip had spent there. They had walked every trail and climbed that fire tower a million times. From the top of the tower, acres and acres of untouched forest lay in view. In the spring blue ash, red oak, black walnut, and honey locust joined hands with hundreds of other native Kentucky trees in a mirage of green patchwork. In the fall, the same trees produced an optical effect with uncountable hues of yellow, orange, red, purple and every shade in between. Colorful, seasonal flora, wax myrtle, and spicebush wafted pungent scents in the wind, filling the rest of the park. Bernheim Forest was God's
nature gift to Bullitt County, Kentucky. And it lazed almost in Abby's front yard.

They walked familiar trails, pitched pebbles into the fishing lakes, watched the circles start small, enlarge, and
then disappear. Abby and Phillip leaned on the old split rail fence, careful not to get splinters in their hands from the aged, unpainted wood rails.

Abby looked around for pens and cages of wildlife which had been injured, treated, and rehabilitated, but there were none today. Rangers used to bring injured animals to the park and nurse them until they

were ready to fend for themselves in the wild again. She fell in love with an orphaned raccoon once and begged the park ranger, who happened to be a neighbor, to let her have it for a pet. Of course, he refused. Said it was wild and he would return it to the wild. Even as a young girl, Abby knew that was best, but she wanted that raccoon.

MsFitZ CAFE

The next Friday when he received his pay for working on a neighbor's farm, Pip brought her a stuffed raccoon, which looked just like Mickey. She had given the live coon a name. The toy one inherited the tag. She owned Mickey after all. So many memories. So many years ago.

They drove around the wooded picnic area, the arboretum, and the duck lakes then climbed to the top of the knoll. Phillip's eyes followed the steps upward to the pinnacle of the tower. Abby glanced at his mischievous face and then at those steps. Was he going to do it? They used to race to the top.

Phillip, with an impish grin, reverted into Pip. His lips spread as he put one foot on the bottom step. Abby whipped around him and planted her toe on the second step, hoisting herself up in front of him and didn't stop more than three or four times until she reached the top. Poor Phillip. He huffed and panted but didn't give up. He wiped the sweat from his forehead. "No fair, you didn't tell me you'd been running marathons."

She giggled like a silly schoolgirl. "No, definitely not marathons, but keeping up with my girls at the café gives me plenty of exercise." She attempted to hide she was breathing hard, herself.

"Well, if I ever get down from this mountain top, I am joining the Y." He stopped three times, catching his breath before finishing his sentence. "I didn't realize how out of shape I am. Guess sitting around all day will do that to you."

"Just comes from having a posh desk job. I think the Y would be fun. I'll join with you if you don't mind." She couldn't believe she'd said that. What if he did mind? Or what if he didn't...?

Phillip picked a brilliant, yellow, golden aster and fixed the stem behind Abby's ear. She trembled at his touch, but turned away and said, "Let's drive back to the grassy picnic area and eat lunch."

"Food is the best word you've said all day. Betcha I can win this contest. I live to eat." He plopped down on the quilt Abby spread over the grass, lifted a corner of the red checked cloth, and peeked into the basket. "Emm— love to smell fried chicken, too." They ate in near silence except for a few awes from Phillip. The couple lingered on the quilt-covered grass. The gold flecks in his hazel eyes caught the sunlight and glittered.

"Gym together? Let's do it."

"Yes, let's do." Her fingers inched across the distance between her hand and his, placing her palm over the back of Phillip's hand. He smiled. She smiled. They sat on the ground, Abby staring out into the distance seeing nothing but blue sky filled with memories, promises, and dreams.

For a few short moments, Abby let her dreams be optimistic. Could it work between Pip and her again? He was a compassionate person. Maybe he could understand about Cynthia. Her fingers glided over the smooth, yet ribbed from age skin of a business executive, as she gently rubbed the back of his hand. Not at all like the coarse hand of a hard-working farm boy. She beamed up at him, wondering if the shimmer of hope in her heart showed in her eyes.

MsFitZ CAFE

They stood to leave, and she thought he was going to kiss her in the middle of the picnic area. A part of her hoped he would, while the other part blushed at the thought of such a blatant endeavor. Still, a thrill ran up and down her spine at the thought of it. Instead of kissing her, he took one of her hands, draped his other arm around her shoulders, and began to waltz. "Abby, I love autumn. The leaves remind me of the ever-changing color of your eyes. First passionate brown, then blazing buttery gold."

"Are we really dancing in the park?"

"Yes, my love, we are waltzing through the autumn of our lives." He smiled down at her and squeezed.

They could waltz through every autumn if only reality would never emanate. Abby met his eyes and swiftly brushed her lips across his. "It's time to clean up the picnic stuff."

They left the park and drove around the area they used to call home. As they passed Jim Beam Distillery, Abby nodded toward the sign advertising Kentucky bourbon. "Is it true that all bourbon is made in Kentucky? Being a tee-totaler myself, I wonder what the difference is."

"Kentuckians like to make that claim. Something to do with no iron in our water and the mash made from homegrown corn. Then the liquor is aged in white oak barrels. I'm not sure all bourbon is made here, but I've heard it is, except for a small place in Tennessee."

A truck, with a round metal container on the back, pulled out of the exit gate of the distillery. Phillip lowered the windows of the Lexus and hooted. "I suppose we lay claim to that stench also?"

Abby threw a Kleenex over her nose and whacked his arm. "Roll that window up! That's one thing I don't miss about living in this part of the county. Don't miss smelling those slop trucks."

Phillip threw back his head and chortled before he pressed the button to close the window. "On that, I totally, whole heartedly agree."

They neared Deatsville Road, and Abby's heart froze. Her pulse pounded on both sides of her head. If only Phillip would turn the car in the opposite direction, staying clear of that bridge behind the distillery warehouses. The relationship between Phillip and her had not reached the point of reliving that one night when Abby lost more than her innocence on the bank of Long Creek. She lost Pip. So much more than water had flown under that bridge.

"If you don't mind, Phillip, I have a slight headache. I'd like to go home now."

His eyes held genuine concern. "I feel like a fool. They've changed these roads. Not sure which one leads out of here." He turned left. "Now I know." He pointed over his shoulder. "There's where they filmed scenes from that movie, 'Stripes.' Never dreamed Bill Murray and John Candy would make a movie in Kentucky." Phillip talked as easily as if she weren't sitting beside him, her heart swelling out of her rib cage, but he didn't know what she did.

Her gaze drifted to his white knuckles. Pip did remember. He was trying to change the subject for her sake. She wished she could tell him she loved him, and the past would disappear into the darkness and hide forever. She wished Phillip would stop the car, pull her into his arms, and kiss away the pain. Why didn't she tell him that's what she wanted—needed? Instead, she said nothing.

They were quiet for several minutes until Phillip pulled his cell from his pocket and read a text, picked up one of her hands, and squeezed it. "Abby, about joining the Y. It may have to wait a few days. I'm needed in Chicago." He turned back toward State Highway 61. "So much for being retired. I might should toss this phone in Long Creek." He looked at her and his eyes softened. "With a little encouragement from the right person, I might do that." When she didn't answer, he stared at the road ahead of him and continued the route home.

Phillip was leaving. A wave of nausea swept over Abby. Her left eye twitched along with the dimpled cheek. Pip was leaving her again. Well, let him leave. After all, leaving was what he did best. They had made love one night by the bridge. Then he left. Only this time his leaving was what she wanted. Yes, she was sure this is what she wanted. Of course, it was. She couldn't offer him encouragement. A woman in her sixties shouldn't rekindle a relationship that didn't work out the first time.

Jean T Kinsey

Chapter Eight

Phillip took the taxi flight to Chicago. Forty-five minutes alone with his inner self gave him time to think. Abby was holding back for a reason. Why? Didn't she believe him when he explained why he'd left without saying good-bye? She should have known he was helpless in the situation or he'd have contacted her. He wasn't the kind of person to use her and cast her aside. Surely, she couldn't believe that of him.

A light bulb turned on inside his head. Why would a young girl, an honor roll student, drop out in her junior year and never return? Why, unless? He toyed with the conjecture for a long time, but that had to be it. Abby had been pregnant. She was having his baby and he was nowhere around. Why did he not see it before? Why would she not tell him now? She'd lost all trust in him, and he didn't blame her. Phillip gripped the armrest of the plane seat. Self-centered, vain, stupid were only a few of the names he called himself. If it were in his power, he'd turn the plane around and head back to Louisville, and to Abby, but that wasn't in his power.

Where was the child now? Had she lost it? Poor Abby. Abortion? Had Abby had an abortion? No, it was against her religion. However, so was getting pregnant without a wedding. His sweet, innocent Abby had suffered all because of him. Because he'd been immature, impatient, and selfish. Now-a-day, it would be different, but not then. Her parents were strict and unforgiving people. He should have been there for her to prove how much he loved her. That was his dad's fault. Not Phillip's. He'd hoped that man rotted in the Eddyville Federal Penitentiary. When the plane landed, he'd go to the office and take care of the problem, then head back to Shepherdsville and insist Abby tell him everything. She'd lived all these years

with her secret, now it was time for him to help her carry the load. At least, he'd be there for her now. If she loved him, she'd understand and forgive him. However, doubts crept in. Abortion? Aborting his baby. He could understand, but could he forgive? Phillip had to stop thinking like that. She had not aborted his child. Abby would not do that. He'd get this business taken care of and fly back to Shepherdsville and to Abby.

The publishing problem turned out not to be a problem at all. The editor of the magazine, "Breaking News," an imprint of Barnes & Barrett, decided to retire after fifty years with the company. Charles Dwight Davidson was stepping down at the age of seventy-six. As President of the company, Phillip would present him with a plaque and a certificate in recognition and honor of a news story he'd investigated in 1971. "Three Sides of Abortion" had won Davidson a Pulitzer Prize and added popularity to "Breaking News" and Barret Publishing. The man, a loyal employee, long before the engraved plaque at Barrett Publishing contained Phillip's name, deserved honor by the company president. Phillip couldn't deny him his due respect.

He called Abby, telling her it would take a few more days than he'd anticipated. He hadn't expected her to sound relieved, but the way she said it was okay, sounded thankful. Maybe he'd misread that kiss. Maybe she didn't feel it as deeply as he did. Could he have seen in her eyes only what he wanted to see? Maybe she resented him more than he'd realized. He'd get busy working on his speech, get his mind on the duty at hand, and flesh out his personal problems later. A few days wouldn't make any difference now.

Articles and reviews about the Pulitzer story covered Phillip's desk. He picked up some back issues of the
magazine and studied the pictures made outside an abortion clinic. He blinked, swallowed, held the paper at arm's length, and pulled the page closer to his face. Yes, the year of the paper was 1971. He pressed the intercom button. "Betty, come in, please."

"Yes, Mr. Barnes." His assistant stood in the doorway.

"I want blowups of these pictures from all angles. Especially of this young girl here." He touched the black and white photograph of the lady in the paper. "Enlarge the wrist where I circled." He pointed at a teenager amid the crowd. "And make it a priority. I need them ASAP."

"Phillip walked to the window. Paced around the room. Sat in front of his desk. Made the entire circuit all over again. Why did it take the woman so long? He'd told her asap.

"Mr. Barnes." Betty tapped on the door and stuck in her head. "I have the blowups you asked for."

"Thank you, Betty." He took the printouts she handed him. "That will be all." She closed the door

behind her, as he spread the prints out on his desk. "No. No. It can't be." He looked at the arm stuck up in the air. A teenage girl with a familiar face and short, dark curls appeared to have come out of the building, trying to cut through the crowd. She held her arm up above her head. The up-reaching wrist had something white around it. The print was fuzzy from over-exposure, but Phillip could make out the shape of a band around her wrist.
A patient ID bracelet? The kind worn in hospitals? He made out a smudgy II. Could it be a partial H for Harris?
The face. He looked again. It was Abby.
"Abby, what did you do? You killed our baby? You should have known I would find you. I tried. If you'd only stayed in Shepherdsville a little longer, I would have found

you. If you had only trusted me," he said aloud. Phillip folded his arms on the top of his desk, dropped his head onto them, and cried. "Why Abby? Why?"
Then he answered. "You fool. You know why. She loved you, and you let her down." That was why Abby devoted so much of herself to those young mothers. She was giving them the support she never got. Clearly, she did not want him to know anything about a child. She still did not trust him. Phillip didn't believe in abortion, but he could understand how Abby must have been overwhelmed with the prospect of caring for a child and herself with no help. Yet, he wasn't sure he could ever look at her again without thinking she had aborted his child. He could have a son or daughter, maybe

grandchildren by now. If he could see inside his heart, blood would be spewing in all directions. Why did he ever go back to Bullitt County?

Phillip put the papers in his briefcase and left the office. He'd finish the presentation in his Chicago flat. Might as well get accustomed to living in that posh, boring apartment again. Shepherdsville, Kentucky wasn't as alluring as it was yesterday.

****

Abby wiped the perspiration off her brow after placing the last pan of biscuits in the oven. Whiffs of sage and an unmistakable smell of fried bacon permeated the kitchen along with brewing coffee. Madison and Chloe bustled from one table to the other, taking breakfast orders from the usual crowd plus several groups of people they'd never seen before. By the time the girls served the last orders, the crowd dwindled to a few lingering stragglers.

Chloe took a deep breath, watched the last customer exit the front door, and gave Madison a high-five. "That's it."

Madison dropped into a booth by the window, kicked off her shoes, and rubbed the back of her neck. "We sure had an influx of breakfasters. What in the world is going on?"

Abby emptied cold coffee from her cup and poured herself a second hot one. "Hope I have time to drink this one while it's still warm." She nodded down the street in answer
to Chloe's question. "Becky Kelley and Ms. Burke were in yesterday. Said they were having a big art show this

morning and some sort of garden party at the Arts Council Building."

"Kelley- that's the lady who wrote the wine book, isn't it?"

"Yes, and Burke is president of the Arts Council." "I had no idea they'd eat breakfast here. However, I'm glad to see our town focusing on the arts these days." Abby nodded her head in the affirmative. "That Bullitt County Arts Center was one of the best things ever happened to the city of Shepherdsville. They're having a luncheon after the showing. And guess who's catering it?"

"You don't mean it. Why didn't you tell me?" Aracella poked her head from the kitchen. "I don't have time to do fancy cooking now." She swiped her forehead. "Si, I feel faint."

"Don't get excited. Ms. Caudill, the VP came in earlier, said they want a simple sandwich and salad lunch. Harper and I are making ham and cheese sandwiches. We baked cookies last night, and the ham is in my apartment oven. We got it covered. Just make some extra salad. We'll serve ice cream and cookies for dessert."

Aracella frowned. You and Harper are getting awfully close. Be careful, Miss Abby."

"And what does that mean? I'm close to all my girls."

"I don't know. It seems like Harper's worming her way into your personal life. Something about her I don't trust."

"When a young girl needs special attention, she gets it in my place. Harper needs me, and I suppose, in a way, I need Harper, too."

"I'm sorry, Miss Abby. I didn't mean anything by it. One day I'll learn to mind my own business."

"Harper's a good girl underneath her rigid exterior. Some children of her race had an extremely hard time growing up here in this county a few years back without seeing a cross burned in their yard. If a black person produced a bi-racial offspring, that child learned to contend with what defense was at hand. Sometimes her only weapon was her tongue, so try not to judge too harshly. I hope to help Harper find a better way than she has known."

"You're right, Miss Abby." Aracella didn't say anything else. Madison and Chloe eyed one another and continued as if they'd never heard the conversation. Madison flexed her shoulder muscles and leaned on the table in front of her. "Miss Abby, can I fix you a plate? Since Mr. Phillip left, you haven't eaten enough to give a nine-day-old kitten enough energy to open its eyes. He's been gone a long time. When is he coming back?"

Abby's cheek creased. "Phillip is away on business. When, or if, he comes back is no concern of mine. He owns a business in Chicago, you know."

Abby pretended to wipe a splatter of coffee off her blouse. "We had a good crowd this morning. Time to take a break before the lunch rush hits you." She pursed her lips. "What about your kids? Have they reconciled yet?"

"Not really. I laid down some rules and they are abiding by them for now."

"Guess that was hard on you."

"Sure was. Both my kids are old enough to form their own opinion, and I can't make them change their minds, but I had to do something. Julianne can have Kyle over when I am home, depending on my class schedule, and he can visit every other weekend, while Noah visits Simon. But that kid, Kyle, is sullen and quiet, a bundle of nerves." Madison shook her head. "Noah goes to his room to play games, watches T V, or finds an activity outside. He's too embarrassed to have his buddies over. Tension in my home is so thick you can slice it up and serve it on a platter."

"Did you speak to the principal?"

"I did, but he said there was not much he could do. Most of the bullying goes on outside the classrooms, and none of the students will tell who did what." Madison tapped her fingers on the table. "I wish I knew how to make this all go away. I don't understand the boy's parents. I couldn't allow my child to go through what that boy does on a daily basis. I'd home-school him first." Anger sparked in her eyes. "And don't you think I haven't considered doing just that. I don't want my children torn apart like this."

The dinging of the bell interrupted the conversation when Julianne stormed through the front entrance of the café. She ran to her mother and threw her arms around Madison's neck.

"What's wrong, Julianne? Why aren't you in school? What's happened?"

Julianne tried to speak, but only whimpered. She made a couple of tries before she wailed. "I told you, Mom. I told you it would happen."

Madison held her daughter by her shoulders and looked sternly into her eyes. "Stop. Breathe. Get control."

Julianne inhaled a deep breath, exhaled, and then spoke. "It's Kyle. He ran away. Mom, I know he'll die out there alone. He's too sensitive to make a way for himself. I had to leave school. I had to, Mom. I have to find him." Tears gushed from her swollen eyes down her puffed cheeks.

Abby poured Madison a cup of coffee and put a straw in a Coke for Julianne.

"I'll help look." Madison slipped an arm around her daughter. "If you can play hooky, so can I. I'll cut classes this afternoon and we'll go out looking for him. Harper will be here soon to help Chloe."

Chloe answered. "Well, butter my biscuits; I can take care of things here. You all go on and search for that poor boy."

"It's all Noah's fault." Julianne sobbed.

Madison rubbed Julianne's hand. "Julianne, you can't blame your brother for everything. This has been looming over all of us for a long time."

"If my brother had not thrown such a fit, Kyle could have been free to talk to me. I could have stopped him. I know I could. Do you want to know what Noah said to me? He said Kyle ran away to be with his own kind."

"We'll ask for prayers for Kyle at prayer meeting tonight. There are some things we can't accomplish on our own."

"Do you really think they'll pray for Kyle? Really now?" She squinted in Madison's direction.

"Of course, we will. Everyone may not agree with him, but we still love him and will continue to pray for him."

"Noah says church people hate all gay people."

"Julianne, that is not true. God is love. If we church goers didn't love, then God wouldn't be in our church, and I assure you, He is. Besides that, you said yourself, you don't even know for sure Kyle is – is like that. I mean you don't know he's gay. Don't you go judging him, too." Madison hugged Julianne. "Now, don't get angry at Noah, God and the world. It's better if we spend our time looking for Kyle."

Julianne sniffled and wiped her nose on a Kleenex. "I need to go home first and get some papers Kyle left at our house. There might be a clue in them. He wrote some deep poetry. Mom, will you go with me?"

Madison looked at Abby, who nodded yes. "Sure will, sweetie. We'll be right back, Miss Abby." The door closed behind Madison and Julianne and opened again as Phillip entered.

Abby's hand flew over her chest. "Phillip."

"Can I talk to you, Abby?"

Her heart leapt into her throat, but she stayed calm. "I have a lot of things to tell you, but we have an emergency. It will have to wait." She explained about Kyle.

"Of course, it can wait. I'll help you search. What can I do?"

Abby gasped. "Harper. She's in the apartment checking on the ham. I forgot about the Art Council Luncheon." She looked at Phillip. "If you really want to help, go with Madison and Julianne. I have to stay here until after one."

When Madison and Julianne returned, Phillip offered to drive them. Julianne made a list of all the places she thought Kyle would possibly go. His parents and the police had probably searched each of them, but it wouldn't hurt to double check. If they had not covered all the spots Julianne could think of, they'd come back to the café, pick up Abby and look some more after the luncheon.

Julianne took a picture from her purse and showed it to Abby and Phillip, so they could recognize Kyle if they spotted him. He wasn't exactly what Abby expected. A frail young boy with a small pixie-face engulfed in blonde bushy hair.

*****

Madison kept a prayer running in her soul. *Please dear God, help us find Kyle alive and well. Please, for Kyle and his family's sake and for my family's sake. This could split my son and daughter apart forever, and I know that is not your will, dear Jesus.* She finished the prayer and started it all over again.

When Phillip turned his car down Hwy 61 toward the bridge, a young boy stepped out and flagged them down. "Noah. What are you doing here?" Madison asked as the boy, covered in sweat from running, slid into the back seat by his sister.

"I've searched the park and the riverbanks. I just came up to check in at the café when I saw Mr. Phillip's car."

Julianne stared at her brother. Ice cubes wouldn't have melted in her mouth. "You have helped enough. Now get out of this car."

"Mom, I want to go with you, but first we need to go to the police station." He buried his face in his hands to catch the streams of water leaking from his eyes. "I may know something."

Julianne cried out, raised her hands, and slapped her brother. He shielded his face with his hands, but he didn't try to stop her. He let her strike him repeatedly. "I'm sorry. I'm sorry," He muttered.

"Julianne. Stop it. Now." Madison attempted to intervene a few times before she gained Julianne's attention.

Noah didn't seem to notice when the slapping stopped. "I didn't mean for anybody to get hurt."

"What do you know, Noah?" Madison said. Julianne's hand stopped, suspended in the air.

"Don't really know anything. I overheard some boys talking. They said they took him somewhere, tied him up, and left him there."

"Who were these boys?" Madison demanded an answer.

"I don't know, Mom. I was in the bathroom stall and they didn't know I was there. I could say I didn't let them know I was there, so I could learn more about Kyle's disappearance, but that would be a lie. I stayed hid 'because I was a coward. I was afraid for me and I was afraid for Julianne."

Madison swallowed. "Why were you scared for your sister? Did they threaten her?"

"Well kind of."

"What did they say about me?" Julianne slowly lowered her hand.

"One of them said you liked gays so much, you must be one. Said something about you getting what you deserved as they went out the door, but I couldn't hear it all. I didn't want anybody hurt. I just wanted to be like the other kids."

Phillip pulled his Lexus into the Government Center back parking lot. He had not said a word until now. He nodded toward the back seat. "You kids stay here with your mom and be quiet. I'm going inside and find a detective I know. I'll get you when he wants to talk with you." He repeated in his non-negotiating tone. "I mean it. Discuss the weather, or how many clouds are in the sky, but do not upset your mother. *Do you hear me?*"

"Yes, sir." They replied.

Phillip opened the door. "I'll be right back. I really don't want anyone to see these two entering the police station."

The occupants of the car sat in silence until Phillip came back. "Noah and Julianne, Detective Mainer wants to talk with you. I insisted he come to your house because it might be chancy if you were seen talking to the police."

"Chancy? Like dangerous chancy?" Madison asked.

We think it might lead to more bullying, and God knows we've had too much of that already. I'll take you home, and I'll drive around the other places where Julianne said he might be if that is what you three want."

"I'd like you to keep looking." Julianne lifted her swollen, red eyes. "Please, Mr. Barnes, Kyle is like a brother." She glanced at Noah. "Well, kind of. Please find him."

"I'll try, but I can't promise you anything. No one can at this point."

Chapter Nine

After the Council luncheon ended and the cafe lunch crowd dissipated, Abby pulled the blue-checked cloths off the tables and put them in the laundry hamper. Neither Phillip nor Madison had contacted her since they left to search for Kyle. She corkscrewed the wet cloth in her hand and straightened it out again before wiping the table. She couldn't help but
worry. Madison was her employee, plus a dear friend. And Phillip--Abby had no idea what to think about him. His few days at the company had turned into ten. She'd begun to wonder if he would ever return when he waltzed through the front door as
 if he'd never left. So many things ran through her head.

Abby played out scenes in her mind. What had happened to Kyle? She pictured a young boy alone, cold, and hungry. Would Noah and Julianne be able to muddle through the strain on their traumatized sibling relationship? A vision
of Madison's children, broken and bitter, flitted before her. She scrubbed at a stain on the table until she realized she was trying to rub off a scratch in the surface.

How would she ever tell Phillip about Cynthia? She must put aside these apparitions and face reality. She must tell him and make him understand. Phillip loved her, but would he, after he heard what she had to say? Even if the movie showing in her head had a bad ending, she knew she must.
Yet how and when? There was so much going on now, maybe she should wait. Timing was important. She

promised herself she'd tell him at the first opportune moment. Before she finished the last table, the bell chimed announcing someone entered the door. Abby froze. Even with her back to the entrance, she sensed Phillip's presence, a palpable force, sucking all the air out of the room.
"Abigail, Madison asked me to tell you what happened today." He used her full name, not Abby. He continued to tell her how Noah flagged them down and how he had hunted all afternoon in vain. Kyle said the boys in the restroom might have mentioned the Bottoms. The police planned to search the Bottoms tomorrow anyway. However, with all the woods, marsh and undergrowth, someone who wanted to hide could do so, and possibly never be found.

Abby tilted her head in thought. They were going into the Bottoms not truly expecting to find Kyle.

"Maybe we should organize our own hunt or volunteer to help with the police search." Abby poured Phillip coffee. "Would you like a sandwich? We have plenty ham and cheese."

He shook his head. "No, we stopped at Frisch's and I convinced Julianne to eat a burger. That kid's in a bad way."

He drank his coffee in silence and put the empty cup on the table. "Are you busy, Abby? I need to talk to you."

What did he want to say that would cause him such distress? His words came from deep inside him, making him hoarse as if they scratched and clawed their way out.

She untied her apron and sighed. Might as well get it over with. Phillip had something he wanted to say. She would listen and then make her confession. The timing would never be fitting for what she had to tell him. "Let's walk down to the City Park. It's nice down there by Salt River."

"Better grab you a jacket. It's also cool near the running water. On second thought, let's drive. We've both had a long day. If we want to walk, we can stretch our legs in the park."

They followed Buckman Street toward the bridge where they turned right and continued on to the park, neither of them speaking, Abby, deep inside her own head, supposed Phillip was also. They parked the car and strolled to the park bench overlooking the Salt River. The crisp breeze rustled the leaves in the trees, and the river water slapped the banks. Occasionally a frog sounded, "Belly-deep." The cheers from the youth football field, partially muted by distance, told them they were not entirely alone.

Abby shuttered and snuggled inside her jacket. She hadn't realized it would be so cold. Phillip slipped his arm around her to shield her from the cool afternoon air. So protective and so warm. She wanted his arm around her forever.

Abby smiled. "It's peaceful to hear the sounds of children playing and having fun."

"Yes, I suppose it is nice. Especially to their parents." His sentence cut so deeply; she had no come back. It was time. She opened her mouth to speak, but Phillip spoke first.

"Abby, I've been in my apartment in Chicago, trying to make sense of our lives. I don't know much for sure, except that I love you and cannot bear the thought of losing you again. However, at the same time, I can't live with deceit. I was on my flight to Chicago when the truth smacked me in
the face. I know Abby. I know." He didn't speak for a while seeming to be waiting for her to confirm his suspicions.
What exactly did he know? What should she admit?
"You were pregnant, weren't you?"
"Disowned you? Your parents? I can't imagine. You should have known I'd come back to Shepherdsville looking for you. I did, Abby. I did come back. You were gone, and no one knew where to find you. I don't blame you for being angry with me."
Phillip stopped talking for a minute. Then found his words again.
Abby froze as the next sentence escaped through Phillips frozen lips. "But an abortion? Did you have to kill our baby? I never dreamed you of all people would be inside the walls of an abortion clinic."
"A-abortion? Pip, I never had an abortion." She tilted her head to search into his eyes. He was serious. "I thought about it, but I didn't."
"So, you still aren't going to tell me. Abby, I can forgive anything except you lying to me. Let's go." Still a gentleman, he helped her from the park bench, but it was hard to follow his long strides back to the car. Why was he so angry? How did he know about the abortion clinic?

Would he ever believe the truth? Did she even want to tell him? If he thought she aborted their child and then lied to him, there was no need reopening closed incisions by confessing the rest of the story now.

The streetlight reflected halos on the light blue Lexus through the side mirror when Phillip parked in Abby's drive, got out of the car, and opened the door for her. "Good night, Abigail."

He was leaving again without giving her a chance to explain. Not that she felt she owed him an explanation. Let him go. She didn't need someone who left at every fork in the road. She pulled her coat tighter and turned toward her steps.

"Abigail, wait." Phillip took something from the glove box. "I prayed you'd explain this to me. I hoped you would trust me enough to know I'd understand. I had to come back. I had to look into your eyes and let you tell me the truth." He handed her a large envelope with photocopies of some newsprint.

"I don't understand. What are these?"

"Now I know why you coddle your young, single moms so much. Guilt is a terrible thing to live with, Abby. Don't worry; I'll continue donating to your cause. Consider it late child support."

"I have no idea what you're talking about."

Phillip continued as if she'd not spoken to him. "I must admit when I first saw that paper, I was angry, disappointed and ready to stay in Chicago, but I kept seeing you alone, scared, and pregnant. You thought I'd deserted you. I had to come back and let you tell me everything. All I wanted was the truth. I just wanted you to confide in me, not tell me more falsehoods."

"I didn't lie to you. I never had an abortion. I was planning to tell you everything tonight. That was before you accused me of deceit. Now you can find out the true story when I feel like telling you. But I must warn you, you won't like it."

Phillip didn't wait for her to finish. He stepped back into his car and sped away spewing gravel from his wheels as he sped out of the back-parking lot.

Chapter Ten

Glad Harper was at her own home tonight, Abby went into the empty apartment alone. Phillip was gone. This time she was sure it was for good. She would miss him terribly, but she wouldn't beg him to stay. If he didn't believe her, then so be it. He probably wouldn't accept the truth any more than the lies he thought she told.

She spread the clippings on the table. Pictures of an abortion clinic surrounded by angry protesters. Abby's eyes fastened on a young girl mobbed as she came from inside the clinic. Someone had drawn a red circle around the face and another around the patient ID bracelet on her up-lifted wrist. Another copy showed a blowup of the bracelet— *oh Pip. Why didn't I tell you everything earlier? Now I fear it's too late for either of us to forgive each other.*

Abby tossed and flipped covers all night, as remembrances from the past played out scene by unnerving scene. First, she relived the shame and embarrassment of discovering she was pregnant, and Pip was gone. Her mother's wails and her daddy's cussing cut like broken glass even now as they rang through her head and she knotted the sheets around her.

She went to live with her Aunt Ruth, the only one who would help her. Aunt Ruth didn't want Abby to get an abortion but agreed to help her with it anyway.

The time finally came, and Abby lay on the white bed, her knees in the air, and her feet in stirrups. Tears streamed from both eyes." " she prayed, but she didn't feel any forgiveness. The nurse, donned in a bloodstained white uniform held a hypodermic needle, ready to inject her. Abby couldn't do this. She sprang from the bed and ran down the hall and out the door, bare foot and in in her surgical gown. She could not end the life nurturing inside her. A life formed by her and the one she loved. A life into which God breathed His own breath.

Now, Phillip hated her.

*****

In the wee hours of morning, Abby finally drifted off to sleep but her eyes popped open at five. Time to continue
her daily routine. Aracella showed a lot of contempt for Harper lately. Since she'd asked Harper to come in early this morning, she didn't want to leave them alone together too long.

Madison came in behind Abby. "I didn't expect to see you," Abby said. "I called Harper in to work a double shift today."

"I went ahead and sent the kids to school. Don't know if I should have or not, but I need to work and maybe school will be good for them. I told the principal about the threats, and he agreed to keep them inside until I picked them up in person. My brain is freezing over. Abby, I can't stand to see my kids in the despondent, angry mood they're in. What about Harper? Do you think she'll mind if I go ahead and work my shift?"

"Harper? No, she won't mind. She's spending the night here anyway. I told her to bring in a few changes of clothing and stay the rest of the week with me."

"You've certainly taken a liking to Harper, Miss Abby. She's taken with you, that's for sure." Madison started breakfast preparation.

"I like to help where help is needed. Guess you've noticed that about me." Abby grinned while reaching for the flour.

"Everybody notices how you treat that young lady, Miss Abby." Aracella piped from the entry door.

Abby's left eye twitched. "I treat her no differently than I do either of you when you need me." She was in no mood to listen to Aracella's obsessions this morning. "Harper comes from a poor home with little education. Both her parents died in an automobile accident. She needs guidance, and it looks as if that lot falls on me."

Madison wrinkled her forehead. "I've always wanted to ask you but was afraid you'd think I was nosey."

"What's that?" Abby said.

Madison continued working. "I know you have a passion for helping single moms, but where does Harper fit in that picture? She's not a mother."

"No, and I'm doing my best to keep it that way."

"I'll say." Aracella piped in. "That girl doesn't need any kids."

"She'll be a good mother when the time is right. Aracella, why do you dislike Harper? Has she done something I don't know about?" Abby directed the question to Aracella, who dropped her head.

"I don't suppose she's done anything. I just get a feeling about some people. You know, when your gut tells you something's wrong, it usually is. Bien, I never saw one of them I could trust."

"Aracella, I know you need this job, but perhaps you might find another one where you'll be happier. You realize Harper's color is not much darker than yours, and it wouldn't matter if it were."

"You know what I mean, she's uh…" Aracella glanced into Abby's eyes. "Are you firing me, Miss Abby?"

Abby bit her lips and didn't answer for a few seconds. "You're a good cook and a great worker, but I don't like friction in my place of business, Aracella. If you can stay on and be happy, we can forget this discussion ever took place. But if not, and you can't tell me anything Harper has done to cause this hostility, then, yes, maybe it would be in
everyone's best interest if you moved on. I'll leave the decision up to you."

Aracella threw her hand over her forehead and said
she might faint as Harper came bouncing through the back door.

"What's wrong, Aracella? Can I help?" She cut her eyes at Madison. "I'll do something nice for her. What can I do?"

"She'll be fine. Give her a few minutes to settle down." Abby scrunched her shoulders.

"Flowers. She likes flowers." Madison printed on a note pad and slipped it to Harper, spelling out f-l-o-w-e-r-s. Abby nodded Madison a silent thank you for getting Harper out of the cafe long enough to get Aracella calmed.

"Okay, I'll be right back." Harper sprinted out the door.

"No need for theatrics, Aracella. Just try to get along and we'll see where it goes." Abby answered.

Soon Harper dashed in the kitchen door, her hands full of bags. "Aracella, I hope you're not too upset. I wasn't thinking when I used so much flour making cookies. I'm sorry. Here's Gold Medal, Pillsbury, and Martha White. I didn't know which flour you liked best."

Abby turned toward the window. She couldn't look at Aracella's shocked face without showing amusement, and Madison followed suit.

"You bought me this because you thought I was mad at you for using my flour?" She held up a bag of Gold Medal.

Abigail and Madison stared with mouth agape while Aracella swallowed Harper up in her open arms. "I have been jealous because you treat Abby with more respect than my daughter does me. Lamento, lo siento. So sorry."

It was good to have peace again in the café, but Abby needed a break. Madison could cover for her, and Harper could do Madison's job. She needed to go up to her apartment and soul search.

MsFitZ CAFE

Chapter Eleven

Madison answered the phone and informed Abby and the others Mr. Barnes was on his way over and wanted to talk to all of them concerning Kyle. Abby stopped instead of going out the door and up to her apartment. So much for quiet, alone time. The same unspoken thoughts must be circulating through everyone's heads. Did he have new information about Kyle? Was he dead? No one said a word. Quiet surrounded them. The icemaker emptied a batch of ice, startling the somber group like a storm alert on a weather radio. Then Phillip entered the door.

Phillip's eyes stopped on Abby for a second as he glanced around the room. His hazel eyes seemed to have softened a bit since last night. She hoped he'd gotten more sleep than she had.

"Okay, listen up." Phillip vied for attention. "I've come from the police station where I had a conversation with Detective Mainer. The police are going to search the Bottoms today. They are open to all the manpower they can get. I volunteered and wondered if any of you might want to do the same." Abby, I wonder if we can use your café as a volunteer base."

"Of course." She nodded. "Anything I can do to help."

"Good. I've assured them we will not interfere with police procedure. They will give the orders and we will follow."

Other citizens wandered in and their voices joined the workers. A policeman came in and Phillip introduced him. "Okay, volunteers, most of you probably know Deputy Jones. He'll be our search organizer today."

While the men discussed their plans, Abby whispered to Harper, "Will you make a closed sign for the rest of the day? We are going to the Bottoms. I've heard about that place but haven't been there in the last forty-some years. The old iron bridge used to be a teen hangout."

"Okay, Miss Abby. I'm on my way." She hesitated a moment. "Just be glad you ain't been there lately and hope you never have to go back. There's been more than one dead body turned up in that devil's playground. I know 'cause I lived near it most of my life." Harper crossed her arms and shivered.

The word passed from mouth to mouth, and many others joined the volunteer squad. The caravan followed the police cars down Cedar Grove Road onto Ridge Road into the river Bottoms. Abby paled at the thought of a child lost in such a vile place. Brown marsh, dead, broken trees, chigger weeds, tickseed sunflower, dried cane and patches of broom sage camouflaged the marshy ground. They had replaced the old iron bridge with a concrete one. Graffiti covered the new bridge. This must still be the spot for local teens to gather. She prayed they gathered to have fun not violence. One could conceal a large animal in the underbrush, let alone a skinny, young boy. She continued the prayer but feared it might be too late to find him alive. If he'd been here since Sunday, he probably wouldn't survive. Yet the people of this county owed him the humane act of finding him, one way, or the other.

The deputy assigned groups and group leaders, pairing each cluster into twos. They would explore every step of land and marsh possible, watching for a movement, a sign of life, or anything out of the ordinary. Each leader carried flares to call for help.

I need volunteers to stay by the cars on each point, so we can pass messages to the other points if necessary. Our cell phones don't get out much down here. No one volunteered. They all wanted to be part of the search. Then Abby spoke. "Come Aracella, this job is important also. We'll man this one." Other ladies volunteered to watch the other checkpoints.

The group leader paired Phillip and Madison in the same group with Chloe and Harper. Each pair would stay together so no one would get lost.

Harper gazed at Aracella. "Now don't you go fainting out here in this bog. I'd sure hate to have to carry you out."

"I won't. Not unless I see a snake or a swamp rat.

"That's what the boots are for. You just don't pass out or I'll leave you for the buzzards."

"Harper, what did I tell you about your mouth? Now apologize to Aracella. Besides, she's staying with me."

"I'm sorry. I was just trying to scare you, so you'd be strong."

Aracella grunted, raised a booted foot, and stepped close to Abby. "I'm fine. Harper was only teasing."

The search party had not gone far when Harper's voice rang through the swamp. "See that burned circle back there in that wooded area."

"What is it? Looks like someone had a campfire." Madison's voice answered.

"Not exactly. I'm telling you; you don't really want to know." Harper answered.

Chloe shivered. "Aracella's not here. You can stop teasing now."

"I'm not teasing. See for yourself. Looks like a goat head burned in there to me. See these signs carved in the tree trunks. A pentagram and an inverted cross. This is a site for devil worshipers."

Chloe looked up at Phillip. "Tell us she's just trying to scare us."

Phillip studied the burned area. "Looks like it could be. Not familiar with these sacrifice altars myself, but it gives me a cold, weird feeling."

"My skin is crawling." That was Madison talking. Abby wasn't unhappy she stayed by the roadside.

"I may pass out. Evil. That's what it is." Aracella made the sign of the cross. "I may pass out." She wobbled on her feet but succeeded to cling to the car.

"I will definitely ask one of the officers to check this out. Now let's get back to searching the rest of the area. Wade through underbrush and thickets. Poke and probe in ever suspicious copse and underbrush." Phillip's voice faded as the group waded deeper into the Bottoms.

A scream from first Chloe, then Madison pierced the quiet. Phillip's and Harper's voices soon echoed through the wilderness.

"Stay here." Abby commanded her cook and waded through the underbrush toward the noises. Madison stood, mouth agape, and Chloe pointed toward the top of a tree, where a body swung from a limb. Phillip shot the flair, so the rescuers would see it. Kyle hung from the top of a dead treetop.

Abby took in every inch of the site. Beer cans lay on the ground around the tree. The end of a long rope hung several feet from the bottom. Footprints mashed the underbrush flat.

Cigarette butts lay on top of the marsh. Right then and there she lost every bite of her ham sandwich.

"How am I going to tell Julianne?" Madison moaned as Phillip extended his other arm around her shoulders.

"We'll help you," he whispered.

Madison wiped her mouth with a cloth, which assured Abby she'd already lost her lunch, also.

Phillip noticed Abby for the first time. "Abigail, what are you doing here? Thought you were out with Aracella. For goodness sake, don't let that woman back here. We'd have to carry her out on a stretcher before we could address the boy."

"She's back at the post. I thought Madison, or someone might need me."

Phillip gathered the women searchers together. "Let's go home now. There's nothing we can do here." He spoke to the detective, who promised to let Phillip know as soon as they put the puzzle pieces together. A series of screams pierced their ears before they left. Mrs. Johnson, Kyle's mother, was in the parking area. The mother cried until she had no strength to cry more. Someone led her to a car.

Madison put her arms around Kyle's mother. "I am so sorry. Please call me if I can do anything at all."

"No one can do anything now." She turned away.

MsFitZ CAFE

"I need to go home and pick up the kids from school." Madison said to Abby.

"Do you want me to go with you?" Abby said, and Phillip echoed.

"No, thank you both, but I need to do this alone." She got out of the car at the café parking lot and stepped into hers, turned left on Buckman toward the light and toward the high school. Abby told everyone to go home. No more work today.

"So, what are you two doing for the rest of the day?" Phillip asked Abby and Harper when Chloe and Aracella left. Abby knew he needed to talk to her, but Harper was upset, too.

"Don't you worry about me." Harper said. "I can go to my room and read or play on my computer. Ya'll go on like I'm not even here."

"Harper, you are here, and you're my guest. I don't think Mr. Barnes will stay long." She raised her eyes toward Phillip expecting him to go. She didn't feel it necessary to leave Harper alone tonight to soothe Phillip's curiosity. She'd tried to tell him once and he didn't listen.

Phillip stayed. "I have an idea," he said. "Why don't we order pizza and I'll run out and get a movie? Harper, you can go with me and pick one you like. I'm not too hip on what teenagers watch these days. I can't even choose one my niece will watch with me, and she's not in her teens anymore."

"That sounds cool." Harper grabbed her purse.

Phillip gave her a high five. Then that's what we'll--," He stopped abruptly. "Abby, is that alright with you? Sorry we left you out of the conversation."

"I don't know. Don't you think it might be a bit disrespectful after what's happened today?"

" Didn't mean to be impertinent. I thought Harper could use a little cheering up."

"Come on, Miss Abby, it'll be fun. I'll even pick out a movie from the dark ages. Did I hear you say something about Paul Newton's sexy blue eyes?"

Abby couldn't help but giggle. Do you mean Paul Newman? Yes, he's my all-time favorite."

"Yeah, I can watch anything. It'll be like a real family. Anything to get our minds off what we saw out there today. Can we do popcorn?"

How could Abby say no? Truth was she didn't want to be alone either. "Fine. I'll stay here in case Madison needs me. You two run along. Get a movie you will enjoy. Newman might be a little dramatic for us tonight, I could use something lighter myself."

Harper stuck her head out the window and yelled as they drove off and left Abby. "Mr. Barnes said we'll pick up the pizza while we're out."

Abby sat out napkins and paper plates. How did she
let herself get in these predicaments? She was happy Harper was spending the night. She couldn't confess anything to Phillip now, with all the visions going on in her head. Not even if she wanted to. Every time she closed her eyes, that young man's form hanging with a noose around his neck, appeared in front of her. Was Madison telling the children now? She should be there with them, but Madison said no. Times like this, families should be together without outsiders interfering. After all these years, Abby still missed family.

Abby slipped into a comfortable pair of jeans and a big shirt. She lay out three bags of popcorn by the microwave. Harper would have her movie and popcorn, and then Phillip would leave, and everyone would get some sleep. Or, at least, try. She doubted if anyone in that rescue crowd would sleep tonight.

Harper's feet pounced on the stairs. She opened the door with one hand and held a large pizza with the other. Phillip trudged behind with the drinks and more goodies for snacks.

Look what we got you, Miss Abby. Long Hot Summer." Harper waved the movie, "With Paul Newman."

"That movie is one of my all-time favorites, but don't think we need anything so intense after the day we've had." Abby glanced at the other disc Harper held. "American Graffiti. That's more befitting for a light-hearted evening. Maybe we can enjoy a few laughs. I love Ron Howard too."

"Suzanne Somers wasn't bad in that T-bird. Wish it'd shown more of her." Phillip grinned. "I urged her to get a movie she wanted to see, but Harper insisted we get something from Miss Abby's time."

"In Miss Abby's era? What about yours?" She pretended insulted. Everyone laughed. It was good to laugh. Harper put the DVD in the player and Abby scooted to the opposite end of the couch from Phillip so Harper with the popcorn, would sit between them.

Before long Harper inched to the edge of the couch. "Miss Abby and Mr. Phillip, did you guys really cruise around in hot cars like that? Man, I dig that Wolfman Jack. Gee, you guys were cool. Is he still alive?"

Abby and Phillip started to speak at the same time, but Abby let Phillip finish. "No, I believe Wolfman Jack died in the nineties. Don't remember what year. Harper, this movie was actually set in California back in the sixties, but in my opinion, it'll always be popular with young and old."

"Well, this is cool anyways." She slid back onto the sofa. Abby could see the fear and anxiety the day had caused, but she didn't say anything. Just gave her an extra-large hug.

Abby liked to see Harper enjoy herself. She really was a child at heart. A child forced to grow up too fast to enjoy being a little girl. She needed to know more about Harper. Why did this little half-black girl appeal so much to her heart?

The movie ended, and Harper excused herself saying she was sleepy. Abby saw through her shenanigans. She wanted to force Abby and Phillip to be alone together. Well Abby had a fix for that. She stood and yawned. I'm sleepy also, Phillip. Perhaps we can talk tomorrow, and then you can be free to go back to Chicago."

"What? Chicago? Remember I have a home in Jefferson County. I plan to stick around for a while. Even if you want nothing else from me, I need to mend our friendship."

She opened the door. "We'll talk tomorrow, Phillip," Abby said as coldly as she could direct her voice to sound.

She supposed she did owe him an answer, but he'd called her a liar. He could suffer through one night as she'd suffered for more than years. Phillip stepped one foot out the door and hesitated. Abby turned to see why, and he kissed her on the cheek. "Good night, Abby. We'll talk tomorrow, and I promise I'll believe every word you say." He disappeared down the stairs. She placed her hand on the burning cheek. Why did she meet up with this man again? She had almost put him out of her mind and out of her heart. Now she really was lying, she'd never forgotten Phillip. Why now at this stage of her life, did he return to Bullitt County? Why did young Kyle have to die?

Chapter Twelve

Abby turned over and slapped the snooze on the alarm clock, but the buzzing continued. What the hey? She pushed the clock aside and picked up the phone.

"Abby, it's Phillip."

"Yes? What? Who?" The readout on the clock showed 4:30am. "Is something wrong?" She didn't believe she could deal with more bad news this early.

"Yes, I mean, no. Abby, I must talk to you. I haven't slept a wink all night. Please, can I come over for coffee?"

"Phillip, Harper is here."

"I know, but can we meet? Can I pick you up and go somewhere?"

"It's awfully early, Phillip."

"Abby, I understand how you must feel about me, but if we have a child, I want to know."

She switched on the bedside lamp, yawned, and stretched her arms. "You're right come on over. Take the steps up to the deck. I'll meet you out there and fill you in with the rest of the story I should have told you before. Then you can re-sort your feelings about me."

She dressed, ran a comb through her hair, and made coffee taking a thermos and two mugs out to the deck along with donuts. Phillip must have called her from his car because he arrived by the time she settled into a chair. Abby nodded and motioned to the cup on the table. He seated himself, neither of them saying a word. Silence changed the space between them from the width of the table to the breadth of a canyon.

MsFitZ CAFE

Abby spoke first, "About the abortion, I really intended to go through with it. Nevertheless, something deep inside me would not let me. Your photographer must have snapped the picture as I bolted out the door. I tripped over a sign and landed on the sidewalk. Someone stepped on my back, and I ended up in the hospital for a few days."

Phillip stirred his coffee. "Sweetheart, I should have been there for you. Was the baby hurt? Were you?"

"Neither of us was hurt badly. I later had a beautiful baby girl. I named her Cynthia."

"Where is she?" Phillip kept his voice low and controlled.

"I planned to tell you at the park, but you didn't give me the opportunity." She picked up a donut, turned it around, stared at it, and then licked the sticky glaze off her fingers.

""Do you think we can ever work it out? Seems like every time I open my mouth; I have to come back and apologize to you for jumping to conclusions." He dropped his head.

"No, Phillip, I don't think we can ever forgive each other. It's not that you weren't here; you couldn't help that. However, I doubt I can ever forget the words you spoke to me in the park. I doubt seriously you will ever forgive me for not telling you the whole story sooner."

He poured them each another cup of coffee from the thermos and ran his fingers through his hair. What could

Abby possibly tell him that would make him dislike her? The abortion thing had caused him anger, but he'd not despised Abby. He could never do that. "Then tell me now. Let's get everything out in the open."

As Abby turned toward the horizon, forcing Phillip's eyes away from hers, he glued them to the scene beyond the city where treetops and rooftops blended in the early morning dawn. She didn't move her eyes from the rising sun and kept her voice composed as if talking to a stranger. "I found a job waiting tables. Went to the free clinic for prenatal care. Aunt Ruth tried to help, but she was old and lived on a fixed income. Just giving me room and board took more than she could afford. I gave birth to Cynthia, but I couldn't make enough money to pay for the things a baby needed to make her healthy and happy. My parents never offered me anything, not even their love."

Phillip pulled a handkerchief from his pocket and silently wiped his eyes. " Abby, if I'd only known."

She crossed her arms. "I didn't know how to get in touch with you."

It might have been easier if she'd yelled the words at him, but her voice remained calm and frostbite cold.

He wanted to hold Abby and say, "I'm here now," but she was across the room looking in a different direction.

Abby continued, "We didn't have WIC and food stamps back then. I was barely eighteen without a high school diploma. Restaurants paid less than a dollar an hour for wages. I was too shy and too pregnant to earn many tips."

Abby articulated each word in the same laconic voice. "My cousin, Connie, Aunt Ruth's daughter, who lived in Bowling Green, came up to visit after I gave birth

my baby. She adored Cynthia. She and Brian couldn't have children, and they visited us often and Cynthia grew fond of them. I tried to be a good mother but saw no way to better myself and make a decent living for Cynthia without finishing high school and college." Her hollow voice showed no emotion as she spoke in run on sentences.
    Phillip swallowed the lump in his throat. He was in college by that time, enjoying life. Yes, he missed Abby, but young men had a way of putting their emotions on the back burner. What a heel he was. She faced the western sky. If she were crying, he could not see the tears, but her blouse shifted lightly around her shoulders, suggesting a faint tremble. Yet, her words spilled out stern and inflexible.
    "When Connie and Brian offered to keep Cynthia until I finished school, I said yes, only if I could see her often.
They agreed."
    Abby turned to face him. Stopped for a moment and rubbed her twitching jaw. "I visited every chance I got. I didn't own a car. The bus went down Dixie Highway with a short stop at Fort Knox. Had to ride the Greyhound Bus for three hours down there and back again plus a layover at Elizabethtown. Nevertheless, I missed Cynthia and needed to see her. Sometimes Brian drove their motorhome to Louisville and parked in Aunt Ruth's drive. When they did that, I saw Cynthia all weekend." She only showed a sign of inner
turmoil when her cheek muscles spasmed.

Phillip clenched the deck rail to avoid reaching out for her. She clearly did not want him to touch her.

Abby stood up and rubbed her back, put her elbows on the rail and turned away from the rising sun. "One Saturday after five years had passed, Connie said she had something to discuss with me. 'Abby,' she said, 'I know how much you love Cynthia, and so do I. Brian and I are having a hard time making ends meet what with paying all the doctor bills, upkeep, and school supplies for her. You know she's been sick a lot lately. I think its allergies and she needs to be on shots. That takes money.'

"I had no money saved. I was working in a department store by then, but didn't make much each week, only working part time and going to school. 'I can send you a little.' I offered but knew it wouldn't be enough.

"Connie had a better idea pending my approval. Said if she and Brian adopted Cynthia, their insurance would pay the medical bills." Abby stared into the brightening horizon.

"My heart bounced up into my throat. 'Adopt Cynthia?' I answered. 'I can't give away my little girl.'"

The word adoption pounded through Phillip's head until it landed in his gut, twisting, and turning.

"Connie promised I could see Cynthia anytime I wanted, and as soon as I was on my feet, she would give her back to me. Adoption was simply a means where they could afford to keep her for me. I had to agree. I believed them. I continued to see Cynthia every time I could save enough money to buy a bus ticket. Then the adoption was final."

Phillip struggled not to sound angry. Abby did what she thought was right. He couldn't remain silent. "Where is she? What happened? They adopted our child?"

Abby met his eyes but continued her story as if she didn't hear him. "I met Paul while spending the weekend with Connie and Cynthia. He was on furlough from Fort Campbell. Like I told you before, we didn't have time for much courting, but Paul liked Cynthia and he loved me. He was a good, kind, man."

Not at all like Cynthia's father. Phillip wished he could have turned back the clock. He should have been the one loving her and the baby. He wiped his nose with his handkerchief.

"Paul said we would adopt Cynthia or whatever we needed to do to make her legally ours. I could live in Bowling Green and go to school at Western Kentucky University. That way it wouldn't hurt Cynthia by pulling her away from Connie all at once. I didn't want to hurt Connie either. But I guess she didn't trust that I would allow her to continue in Cynthia's life." Abby wiped her eye with the back of her hand. Phillip stood dead still.

"Cynthia called Connie Mama, and she called me Mabby, her combination of Mama and Abby. I would have lived in Bowling Green so Cynthia could be with both of us."

"That's because you are a good person, Abby." Phillip whispered.

"You can say that after I gave away our baby?"

He needed to take her in his arms and hold her, but she stood in a frozen trance with her arms locked around her bosom as if protecting herself from his touch.

"I don't know. I only know I went to see Cynthia and they were gone. The house locked tight, and the motorhome gone. No one, not even Aunt Ruth, knew where they were. By then, The Army had shipped Paul off to Nam. He promised to help me find her as soon as he got home, but then he never came home. Cynthia never got to carry his name."

Phillip's face, turned toward the white cumulus clouds behind him, breathed in a short wisp of air. "Nor mine," he whispered. "Then you don't know where Cynthia is?" He asked aloud.

"No. Now you can hate me if you want to. I gave away our child." Her calmness dissolved as she sat at the table, put her head on her folded arms, and wept.

"You didn't give her away. They tricked you. Probably planned it from the beginning."

Phillip fingered the short curls on the back of her head. "I could never hate you, Abby. I love you. Sure, we have a past to overcome, but don't give up on our future."

She raised her head and stared into his face. "There's no future for us, Phillip. Can't you see that? I try to make amends by helping other single moms, but no matter how much I give to others, I can't make up for giving away my baby."

"Then we will find Cynthia. Together, we can find her, Abby."

"It's too late now. I used to pray I would hear you say those words, but it's been too many years. I did

MsFitZ CAFE

everything possible to find Cynthia but found nothing. I'm sure they taught her to forget about me."

"Listen to me." He tried to put his arms around her, but she shrugged him away. "We don't know that until we try. Write down everything you remember about Connie, Brian, and Cynthia. Every single little detail. Tell me everything you know about that motorhome. If they belonged to any travel clubs, anything, no matter how minimal you may think it is. And birthdays. Do you know Cynthia's Social Security number?"

"We can't find her. It's been years." Abby shook her head no. "I won't put myself through that agony again. Don't you understand? I wore blisters on my knuckles knocking on doors and lost my voice on phone calls. Even more so, my heart still has open wounds in it. I can't go through that again. Evidently, she doesn't want to be found. I've never left Shepherdsville; in the hope she might someday come looking for me. It's too late. Just too late." She covered her face with her hands and wept more. "I gave our baby away!"

"I don't know, Abby, I only know I have to try. I'll hire the best detective agency this side of the Rockies. Don't quit on Cynthia and don't quit on us."

"Search all you want, but I have to open the café. I'll need to go through some papers and have a list for you by the end of the day."

"Take as much time as you need. A few hours won't make a difference now," Phillip said.

*****

Abby went through the motions of running her café, but her heart was not in it. She finally left the cleanup after breakfast to the staff and went upstairs to her apartment. Surprised at the memories they brought back, Abby pulled out old papers and photos. She even remembered the color of Brian's eyes. Almost charcoal gray. After she comprised the list and put pictures in an envelope, she sealed it and wrote Phillip's name on the back. She returned to the café, gave instructions to the girls to put the envelope by the register so they would give it to Phillip, then got in her car, and drove away. She had a lot of thinking to do. She hoped Phillip \would find Cynthia but doubted that very much. A few days alone would do her good. She headed down 61 South with no destination in her mind. She needed to be alone.

Abby ended up at the old farmhouse where she grew up, the place where she and Pip enjoyed each other for so many years, so long ago. Was that why she came here? Of course not. She simply wanted to be alone. She rooted around and found a blanket stored away in a closet and prepared her bed for sleeping before dark pushed all the sunrays out of the house.

Why didn't she think to bring candles? Not that it mattered much. Dark wasn't so bad. It didn't take external light to see the inside of her soul. She wouldn't like what she saw any better in the hours of daylight.

This old home held so many memories. Most of \which, she held fondly in her heart. Her loving mom who kissed away all her little cuts and scratches and the stern, yet gentle dad, who taught her to be the tomboy she was. She couldn't understand how these near perfect people turned into the cruel, hard-core parents who turned their daughter away when she needed them most.

Abby ran her hand lightly over her mom's old chest. A drawer popped open. The same hidden drawer her mom used to open and tell Abby the family kept all their secrets hidden there. They laughed together because there were no family secrets back then.

However, this time the drawer contained numerous envelopes. She reached to pick up one, but suddenly drew back her hand. She didn't know why. She had to stop before touching that letter. Abby wished her mirror-self were there. She could use another face to talk with. Finally, she said aloud, "Abigail, stop being foolish, a paper envelope can't hurt anyone." Yet a rattlesnake curled up in that drawer wouldn't have frightened her more than those yellowed envelopes. Pushing premonitions aside, Abby took out the whole bundle of letters. The first one was addressed to Abigail Harris in care of Ruth Mitchel. What was this? Had Mom and Dad not hurt her enough? Did they feel the need to continue shaming her on paper? She already knew how they felt about her. She scooped the letters up into a Walmart bag and stuck them in her suitcase. She'd destroy them later. No need for anyone else to discover the Harris family secrets.

Chapter 13

Harper scooped first regular and then decaf into the top bins of the coffee makers. "Anybody heard from Miss Abby?"

"No, and tomorrow is Wednesday." Chloe wiped off the counter.

Madison sighed. "I for one will be glad when she gets back. It's not easy to get here at five, make biscuits, prepare the hash browns, then go home and drive the kids to school."

"I thought your kids walked to school," Aracella said.

"No, she takes them now after the incident in the Bottoms." Harper checked the cash register before the customers arrived.

"I don't let them out of my sight, especially this early in the morning except for school and I worry about that." Madison hung her apron on the hook and hastened out the door calling over her shoulder, "Be back in twenty."

Harper bustled around the café making sure everything was in place. "Can't blame her for protecting her children after that happened to that boy. Especially since she never did find out who made that threat toward Julianne. Wish I could get my hand on that young man. He'd think twice before threatening her again."

"They never arrested anybody for the hanging either. I'd keep my kids tied to my apron strings." Chloe pulled at her hemline as it crawled up her legs when she leaned forward to pour the gravy in the steam table. "Butter my biscuits; I was hired to be a waitress, not a cook."

In defense of Miss Abby, Harper answered. "We are supposed to be whatever Miss Abby wants us to be while she's gone. Sure hope she's all right. I never seen that lady so down in the dumps as she was when she left here Friday afternoon. We need to shake our tails and get this café hopping by the time she gets back."

"And when do you predict that might be? I need a day off to visit with my son." Chloe wiped her hands on the towel flung over her shoulder.

Harper poked her head through the opening over the grill. "I'd venture to guess she'd be here today or early tomorrow. Miss Abby won't let anyone make her dumplings save her own self, and Wednesday is chicken and dumpling day. I look for her any minute."

Aracella giggled. "You're probably right. I wouldn't know where to start. Sometimes I think I know what seasoning she puts in them, but again, I'm never sure and she won't tell." She whipped up the scrambled eggs.

Chloe swung her hips in route to unlock the front door for the converging crowd. Madison sprinted through the door.

She'd forgotten to ask someone to check on the biscuits in the oven, but Harper lifted them out brown and crusty just in time.

Madison announced Miss Abby had called her. She wouldn't be back until Saturday. "Said either Aracella or I can make the chicken special. Do you want to try?" she asked Aracella.

Aracella shook her head so hard a sprig of hair fell out of her up do. "Not me. I don't do dumplings."

"That's okay. I'll do them. Simon texted me. Wants to drop by and talk after lunch. He chose Wednesday, so he could get Miss Abby's chicken and dumplings." Madison sniggered. "I'll make an extra batch especially for him. On the other hand, maybe I'll cook some stew. He loves my stew."

For the Wednesday special, Madison decided on the stew–nice, juicy, dark stew. Simon's favorite. Customers wouldn't like her dumplings anyway.

Chloe slanted her head and glanced quizzically at Madison. "Don't you go letting yourself in for another hurt. You know how cruel that ex-husband of yours is, and the entire time making you think he's doing something nice."

"You don't have to tell me anything about Simon. I know how to cope with him."

"Sure, hope you do." Chloe murmured. I wish you'd turn that iPod down. It's getting on my nerves."

"I will soon as I take care of this little task."

;Madison loved the soundtrack from the movie *The Help* almost as much as she did the movie itself. June Carter and Johnny Cash, Bo Diddley and Chubby Checkers took her back to the sixties. *The Help* held a special meaning for her, especially for today.

Simon, her ex, waited at the table. She had an inkling of what he would say. Madison donned her prettiest smile and sashayed toward him. She placed the stew on the table in front of Simon. "Now what was it you wanted to discuss with me?"

He stared into the water glass he twisted around in his hand. "Well I guess you heard about Lisa and me." He lifted his eyes slowly to meet hers.

"Yes, Noah told me. Sorry about that. It's a shame you two couldn't make it together, especially with a child coming. I heard she was pregnant." Madison bit het tongue in an attempt not to snicker. He deserved what he got.

What did he want from her? She let her eyes run over his ruggedly handsome face. Simon could have any woman he wanted, and he had chosen her. Pride used to exude from her when she introduced her husband to a friend or when she saw women eyeing him while they thought she wasn't looking. She didn't mind because he was hers. She loved his looks and she loved Simon. But that was years ago. She would not fall for his looks and charms again.

"If you remember correctly, I can't father any more kids after that surgery. Yeah, she was pregnant all right, but not by me."

"That thought crossed my mind," She wanted to giggle aloud, but covered her lips in pretense of a cough. "What's that to do with me?"

He reached for her hand and she slowly inched it away. "Madison, I don't know what happened. I think I was going through a mid-life crisis. I'm sorry for the way I treated you." He looked at her with his sad, puppy dog eyes that once melted her heart. "Could we talk?"

"I guess we should talk but let me think about it for a few minutes while you eat. Here's some hot corn bread to go with your stew." Her lips spread across her face as Simon's green eyes lingered over hers. "Miss Abby didn't get home in time to make her special dumplings, so I made some beef stew. Hope you like it. It used to be your fava."

Simon stirred the food she sat before him. "You were always a good cook, Madison. I'm sure it's fine. Looks a little darker than usual." He pecked at a black speck with his fork.

"That's because I added brown gravy with seasonings. Darkens it up a bit. A little garlic, too, and pepper. Miss Abby has this new pepper grinder."

He took a bite and chewed slowly on first one side of his mouth, then transferred the food to the other side and chewed more. "A little sweet and garlicky, but you did good." He nodded then rested his spoon in the plate.

"Go ahead and eat up, so we can talk." Madison placed her hand on his arm and let it slide gently toward his hand.

He took another bite, chewed extensively, and swallowed, gulped, and quickly wiped his mouth. "I'm sorry, dear. This is delicious, but I'm just not hungry today. Too much on my mind. Let's discuss our situation. Do you think we can stop lashing out at one another and try to mend our relationship?"

MsFitZ CAFE

"I suppose I can try to put the past behind." She ran her finger up his arm this time. "Simon, I'm glad you ate my stew. I made it just for you. You've been feeding me bull for eighteen years. Thought you might like a taste of it yourself." She stared at the half empty bowl.

Simon's eyes enlarged to golf ball-size. "Madison, what did you do?" he spoke through ribbon-like lips and ogled the stew.

Madison's face lit up bright as the neon MsFitz sign. "Do you remember Minnie's chocolate pie in "The Help"? Well, I visited the barnyard and scooped up a cow patty."

Simon's face turned gray. "You didn't? You wouldn't! Did you?"

"No, I didn't, or yes, I did. Take the answer of choice, for you'll never know for sure."

Simon, now avocado green, covered his white lips with a handful of napkins and ran for the men's room, bumping into tables and scattering dishes as if the bull itself had invaded the café.

Harper bent over in laughter. "Well, I wish Miss Abby could've seen that."

"She did! It was hilarious." Abby had slipped in the back door and silently stood behind the workers.

"You are back!" Harper smiled from one pierced ear lobe to the other.

Sounds of surprise and welcome rang from the rest of the gang.

Abby joined in the laughter. "Madison, did I tell you how much I admire you? But please tell me you did not serve that stew to any of my regulars."

"No, I concocted that solely for Simon. I thought he deserved a special batch made just for him." Madison giggled as Simon, handkerchief covering his mouth, slinked out the door.

Abby was glad no customers were in the café to witness the incident. She asked no one in particular, "Did Phillip come by for the envelope I left him?"

"Yes, he did," Chloe answered. I handed it to him personally. "He sure seemed down. But he wrote you a note inside this envelope." She handed Abby a business-size packet, which she opened and silently read.

Dear Abby, Sorry I missed you, but then, I will always miss you. I won't pester you with annoying phone calls or visits, but please remember I am here if you need me. I promise to let you know when I find Cynthia. Enclosed is a document for you to sign and return to the bank. I have set up a trust fund for your girls. Please stop and contemplate before you refuse it. I want to help with the mommy fund for the same reasons as you. If we can help single mothers keep their children, maybe it will ease our guilt over our Cynthia. I am aware my self-reproach has not tortured me as long as your anguish has plagued you, but my remorse is just as real and burns as deeply, for the true blame lies on me. Please allow me to assuage my conscious. Cynthia is my daughter also. We will find her, Abby. This is one promise I will not break.

Love Phillip.

Abby folded the note and put it back in the envelope. She couldn't deny the girls the advantages the trust fund could give them. Maybe she and Phillip could work together on this. They didn't have to be "together" to coordinate a joint venture. Especially if they lived in different states. She wondered if Phillip had returned to Chicago or if he was in Louisville. She shrugged. It didn't matter. She would avoid seeing him again wherever he was.

Abby turned her attention to her girls. "Hey, ladies fill me in on the local happenings. What's going on with Kyle's case, Madison?"

"Nothing, as far as we know. I haven't heard about any arrests, and Detective Mainer promised to let me know if they solved it. You know, since this thing has so deeply affected my kids, he likes to keep me informed. Hal thinks I should get Noah into a bully prevention program at school."

"Oh, Hal it is. I see." Chloe teased.

Madison swatted a towel at her. "No, you don't see."

"Why, Madison, do I see a blush on those cheeks of yours?" Chloe continued to josh.

"You know me better than that. Once burned is enough for me. You saw us having dinner at the Ponderosa, but that was only to discuss the kids."

"I see, too," Harper joined the teasing.

"You two are too nosey for your own good. I told you, I don't plan to get close to a man ever again. Right, Miss Abby?"

"You're not getting me involved. I can't tend to my own affairs let alone get involved in someone else's." Abby avoided the tête-à-tête.

"Speaking of which," Harper said. "Ain't you and Mr. Phillip ever gonna make up?"

"Watch that grammar, Harper. I haven't been gone a week and you've forgotten all I taught you." Abby changed the course of the conversation. "Madison, how are Julianne and Noah? I've been worried about them."

"I don't know. Neither of them talks to me about it. They're both going to Seven Counties for counseling. Noah has formed a bully prevention club at school. Juliane still avoids being part of anything pertaining to Noah."

"That is so sad. The whole situation is unbelievable. How could anything so horrendous have happened right here in Shepherdsville? I saw the judge executive today on the noon news. Reporters interviewed her about the case. She reflected how sad the whole county is and said they were holding a county-wide memorial service for Kyle next Saturday."

"I don't know her?" Harper asked.

Madison smiled one of the few smiles she had lately. "The Judge Executive. You must be one of the few people in Bullitt County who doesn't know her. She is always busy and involved."

"Saw the state senator ordering flowers at the flower shop yesterday," Chloe said. "Probably for the memorial, considering the large order she placed."

"Looks like the whole town's on edge, and rightly so. Do you think things will get back to normal around here?" Madison asked.

Abby wrinkled her forehead. "What's normal?"

MsFitZ CAFE

Chapter 14

Madison dried her hands with the dishtowel and tried to ignore the eerie growling in the pit of her stomach about
the visit she'd promised Kyle's mom. She'd given her word Julianne could go to see her when the counselor thought she was ready. He'd finally given his permission.

Counseling at Seven Counties had helped Julianne and Noah regain some buoyancy. They even smiled occasionally, but not at each other. Detective Hal Mainer in his helpful, unofficial manner, offered to go along. Julianne wasn't too keen on that idea. "Mom, it's not I don't like him, but this is personal," she whispered.

Madison asked Noah to go also, and to her surprise, he didn't fight it as hard as she expected. He hung his head and stammered, "Can't you just tell her I'm sorry? I am, you know."

"No, Mom. Just us. She doesn't need to see Noah right now. If you must have someone to support you, ask Miss Abby. I think Mrs. Johnson knows her."

Hal and Noah dropped the ladies off at the Johnson's drive in front of the two-story Cape Cod, where a tall, middle-aged lady stood at the door. A loose strand of blond hair hugged Mrs. Johnson's sallow face while her eyes tracked each of the three ladies who stepped out of the automobile. "I don't suppose your friend knows anything else about who killed my boy?"

MsFitZ CAFE

"No, I don't think so but they're still working on it," Madison answered.E

"Now I want to speak to Julianne." She put her arms around Julianne. "Thank you, for being a friend to my Kyle. He loved your family very much. Come on in. Don't give the neighbors something else to gawk at." She led the way into her home. They stepped into the foyer and followed Mrs. Johnson into the plush-carpeted living room.

Madison smiled politely." So, Mrs. Johnson, what did you want to talk to Julianne about?"

Mrs. Johnson stared at Abby.

"Oh, I'm sorry. I thought you knew each other." Madison started to introduce the two ladies.

"We do." She continued to look at Abby.

Abby reached out her hand with no response from the other woman. "I know you didn't expect to see me here, Grace. However, I assure you I'm not nosing into your business. Madison is a good friend and needs my moral support. I can wait in the kitchen while you talk. She can find me if she needs me." She turned toward the kitchen.

Mrs. Johnson shook her head no and motioned them all to sit. She rubbed her forehead. "Need to explain something to Julianne about Kyle. I only want her to know."

"But Mrs. Johnson...." Madison interjected.

"Call me Grace, please." The lady attempted a limp smile.

"Sure, Grace, and I am Madison. I wanted to say it's not that I don't trust you, but Julianne has been through a psychological challenge. You can understand that. Kyle was her best friend."

Mrs. Johnson nodded in agreement.

"Then you must understand, Grace, I know you wouldn't deliberately hurt her, but she is in a delicate frame of mind. If you need to talk to her about Kyle, I am going to be right by her side. Miss Abby can go out, but I am with my daughter." She took Julianne's hand.

Julianne removed her hand and placed it on her mother's shoulder. "I wish everyone would stop talking like I'm not here. I can speak for myself, and I want to know anything that will help me understand about my friend. Mrs. Johnson, if Mom can stay with me, it would make her feel better."

Grace fluttered her hand. "I suppose they both can stay. Makes no difference now, anyway."

Grace half-closed her eyelids and turned to Julianne and her mother. "This is hard to discuss, but I think it will
help you understand Kyle better. Some called him gay. Others used uglier names. Not sure what gay means exactly, except I used to think it meant happy. Happy did not describe my
boy."

"Gay or not gay, Kyle was my friend." Julianne answered.

Mrs. Johnson bit her lower lip and waited before she continued. "I know dear, but there's more. Didn't you ever wonder why he didn't hang out with other boys?" She moved the toe of her shoe in small circles on the floor. "Do you
know what a hermaphrodite is?"

"I-I'm not sure." Julianne said.

Madison scooted across the velvety upholstered sofa and grasped her daughter's arm before she addressed Grace. "Where are you going with this?"

Grace kept her eyes on Julianne. "Another word for hermaphrodite is intersex. That's when a baby is born with both female and male organs."

Julianne and Madison simultaneously let out a whoosh of breath. Julianne whispered, "Was Kyle…"

Grace kept talking. "In my early pregnancy, ultrasound told us he was a boy. You should've seen the pure happiness gleaming from Kyle's daddy, Galen's face. He wanted a boy from the very beginning. He went out and bought blue everything a baby boy could possibly use. Even went as far as purchasing a blue and white Kentucky basketball."

Words rolled from her as if she had held them back so long, they now burst through a barrier. "But when I gave birth to him, Kyle came to us half boy and half girl. The doctors said surgery would correct him and advised us to wait until he was older, perhaps until puberty to see which gender he favored. Galen would have no part of that. Since God gave him to us with the male organ more pronounced, he insisted the doctors "fix" his *son* soon as possible. No child of his would go around not knowing his own gender. He wouldn't be welcome in either the girls' or boys' restrooms." Her voice broke and she continued in a gravelly whisper. "Ironically, he said Kyle'd be a laughingstock, if he didn't have surgery as soon as they could schedule the operation."

Madison, Julianne, and Abby wiped away tears streaming down their cheeks. Grace went on to tell them how the doctors did surgery as a baby, removing some parts and rebuilding others. They started injections of male hormones when he2a9 was twelve.

Madison's heart played skip-rope on the walls of her chest. The poor child. Poor Kyle.

Julianne abruptly sat down and buried her face in her hands. Her cotton blouse rippled as her shoulders shivered under it.

Grace stared out the window above their heads. "When he was about three, Kyle found a rag doll some child had left here. He named her Jody. He cuddled her, rocked her, and sang to his baby. He even slept with baby doll, Jody. In his child's voice, he peeked from under his blond, curly eyelids, and said, 'When I grow up, I want to have lots of babies.' How could I take his baby away from him? I let him play with Jody until his daddy found him rocking her and threw Jody in the garbage."

Mrs. Johnson crisscrossed her arms over her chest and squeezed her upper arms until they turned red. "Galen didn't mean to be cruel. He thought he was teaching Kyle how to be a boy." She turned her back to her guests. "But as he grew up, his body did not conform to a male stature. He was short, blond, small, and had a pixie face. Doctors said
that was rather common in such cases" She shook her head slowly. "I'm sorry, I need a rest. Can I get you something to drink?"

Julianne jumped to her feet. "You sit down. I'll get u
for Grace, Madison, and Abby, and fixed herself a Coke.

Madison, sorry she'd waited this long to allow Grace to share the millstone hanging around her neck, attempted to make polite conversation, but Grace continued talking about Kyle. "Galen wanted him to be a normal little boy so badly. He insisted Kyle put his hands in his pockets when he talked in hopes it would break the feminine habit of fluttering his hands and fingers. He never allowed Kyle to giggle." Grace placed her hand over her heart. "Galen said it was an abomination for his son to be too girly." Madison turned her head so as not to show the revulsion. One look at Julianne, and she feared her daughter might retch up her coke.

"Once, when Kyle was about seven, I was resting on the sofa. He thought I was asleep, but through the corner of my eyes, I watched him go into my bedroom. Through my dresser mirror, I saw my little boy go to my chest and pull out a silk nightgown and tie a scarf around his waist to hold it on." She wiped her eyes and added, "He had thrown such a fit when I tried to get his hair cut, I let it grow as long as Galen would allow. My little boy brushed his hair toward his face and tied a ribbon in it, then prissed in front of the mirror. I saw something in his face I had not seen since his dad disposed of Jody— pleasure."

This was getting too deep. Madison excused herself to go to the restroom. After she freshened herself, she forced her feet to walk back into that living room. She must get Julianne out of there. How would such dark information affect her already fragile daughter?

Julianne sat trance-like, not bothering to dry her wet cheeks. No wonder Kyle was such a sad boy. How could his parents have done this to their child? She sat beside Julianne and hugged her. Abby stayed politely quiet.

"Did--Did Kyle know?" Julianne murmured.

Mrs. Johnson folded her lips inwardly around her teeth, paused, breathed deeply and replied, "Yes, I took him to the doctor, who explained his condition before giving him the shots. I couldn't see the hormones helped except he grew more pubic hair, and his voice changed.

"Before the--the incident in the Bottoms, I convinced Galen we had made a big mistake. He didn't want to believe it, but he had no other choice. Kyle slipped away from us daily. We went back and learned from the doctor the surgery could be reversed. Kyle, reluctant at first, admitted he needed to be a girl. Pretending to be someone he was not demanded too much."

Julianne quietly squeezed her eyes shut and clamped her teeth onto her thumbnail. Madison whispered. "I think we should leave now." Julianne shook her head no.

Mrs. Johnson cleared her throat. "He wanted to wait until after graduation. They could do the operation after high school and maybe stay out of college a year while he made his transformation. It would save humiliation, and he would tell no one outside the immediate family except Julianne." Relief from allowing this secret to escape from the depth of her soul reflected in the sad lady's face.

Madison thought she had problems. Her problems were minor compared to what this poor, frail mother had carried for seventeen years. She silently prayed for peace. Grace stared down at her folded hands and finished through trembling lips. "Then all the bad things started. My baby gave up. He just gave up." She sobbed. "Then they killed him."

Julianne flew to Mrs. Johnson and flung her arms around her neck. "I wish he had confided in me. Maybe I could have helped."

"He didn't like to talk about his condition, and you did help, my dear, by being his friend just the way he was." She dabbed a Kleenex to her eyes.

There wasn't much more to talk about. Even small talk seemed out of place. They called the guys from Abby's cell and left Mrs. Johnson with her remorse and her grief. Abby hoped her burden was a little lighter after sharing it. No wonder the poor woman needed to tell somebody. Madison didn't see how Mr. Johnson looked at his own face to shave mornings. Nevertheless, he must be suffering also. Guilt is a hard load to carry. She squeezed Julianne's hand. "Are you okay?" she asked when they were in the car.

"Yeah, I think so. I understand Kyle a lot better now. Myself, too. He was my best friend. We talked about things I should have only confided to my closest girlfriend. I sometimes wondered if I had a problem."

Madison related to Noah and Hal what Grace told them. Noah cleared his throat and coughed several times. Then he stopped attempting to hide his emotions and cried aloud. Even Hal dabbed his eyes.

"Thanks for telling me, Mom." Noah sniffled.

Julianne shot a sharp remark at her brother. "Does it make you feel like even more of a heel now?"

"No. Nothing could make me feel worse. I judged him when I should have offered him friendship," Noah spoke as much to himself as to anyone in the car. "Every night when I try to go to sleep, I see Kyle hanging from that tree." He sobbed aloud. "I'm sorry, Jules." He leaned his head against the side window.

Julianne stared at her brother. "I think I believe you, Noah."

"Jules, I still gotta be upfront with you. I don't believe it's right for a normal person to choose his own sexuality." He bit on his fist and looked out the window. "But I won't ever again intimidate anybody else? Who am I to judge anybody? That's God's job."

Chapter 15

"Sure is good to have a peaceful day around here for a change," Harper straightened the menus and restocked the dishes with packets of sugar, appreciating this morning
started off in a slow and easy manner. Unhurried customers arrived in soft-spoken chitchat groups. It made Harper's job easier and since she had more time to decipher Harper's scribbling on the order pads, Aracella was in a jolly mood.

"Yes," Aracella replied as she peeled potatoes for the stew in preparation for lunch. "Looks like most of the drama has settled. Miss Abby seems to be getting back to her old
self again."

"Seems that way to most people, but I still see Mr. Phillip's image in her eyes. She's not as happy as she pretends."

"Shhh, here she comes." Arabella nodded toward the front entrance.

Abby came in the front way as Madison entered the back door. "Thanks, Harper for covering for me. I'll be finished with these classes one day."

"Madison, are you going to graduate soon? We'll throw you a big party." Harper's eyes sparked with happiness for her friend. She fingered the saltshaker. "Wish I was smart enough to graduate from college."

Abby answered before Madison had the opportunity. "Harper, I told you if you want to go to college, you can go. I was waiting for you to give me an answer. All it takes is the want to."

Harper's eyes dropped. "Ah, Miss. Abby, you know how it is with me. You know I'm not smart enough. "

"And you heard what I said about you talking bad about yourself. If you want to go to college, we'll get you there. If it takes a tutor to prepare you, well, we can do that, also. Think about it and let me know."

Harper bit her upper lip. "You know how much trouble Aracella has trying to read my food orders. And sometimes, somebody must figure the prices for me. It would be a task to teach me anything."

"I know you have difficulties, but don't forget I was a teacher for several years. I have a special needs teacher friend I'd like you to meet. She was once a special ed student herself, and now she is a teacher. And a good one at that. If you're serious and are willing to work at it, let me know."

Harper kept her head bent as she refilled the salt and peppershakers and wiped them off. "I'll think on it. I really will." Could she do that really? Go to college and all? It would be like living in a dream. A real fancy dream. She touched her lips softly. "Was that teacher as bad off as me?"

Miss Abby gave her one of those sweet little smiles. "Yes, Harper, let me know when you decide."

MsFitZ CAFE

Madison's cell phone startled them out of the conversation. She motioned for them all to come closer and whispered around the phone. "It's Hal. He has news about the hanging. He'll be here in a few minutes." The café got quiet. Goose bumps popped up on Harper's skin as they always did before she got bad news. Nothing good ever came out of them Bottoms. She froze when the detective entered the diner. Had the police found a voodoo doll down there in the devil's playground? Her Aunt Nellie had told her about such goings on. Harper needed to come up from her deep wonderings or she would miss the detective's details. Something about three boys coming in and confessing.

"So, did they kill him? I mean murder him in cold blood?" Harper asked.

Miss Abby shushed her. "Let Detective Mainer speak. We can ask questions later."

Hal continued. "Sorry I couldn't let you guys in on this sooner, but you know how police procedures go. Three high school juniors came in last week and told their story. Crime scene investigators checked it out and we're satisfied they're telling the truth."

"What happened, Hal?" Madison said.

"According to the boys, they were only trying to scare Kyle and things got out of control."

"Out of control? That's quite an understatement. How did things get out of control more than they already were? The poor kid was hanging from a tree." Madison all but yelled. "Out of control my eye."

Abby chewed her bottom lip, and her left eye blinked. Aracella's hand squeezed Harper's arm.

"I know one thing; they were three scared kids. According to the parents, the boys couldn't sleep or eat. When parents pressed them, they fell apart and admitted everything." Hal went on in his usual calm voice. "The boys tied a rope around him and pulled him up in the tree. Then slipped the noose around his neck and tied the other end to a branch. They forced him to look down at the ground. Taunted him about how far he would fall before the rope snapped his neck.

"We questioned each of the boys individually and alone. They each described the same scenario. The crime scene lab checked the statements against the evidence. Length of rope burn marks on neck. Lack of burn marks on Kyle's hands. Everything corresponded. Kyle had not clenched his hands around the rope in attempt to keep from choking."

Harper couldn't stand it any longer. "Tell us what happened. Who pushed him out of the tree? Why didn't he grab the rope and pull himself up?"

"Harper, I can't give you names. These boys are underage. They swore no one pushed him. When they forced him to look down, he used his heel to push off and swung himself out into space with the rope around his neck." The detective spoke calmly but his Adam's apple protruded between sentences. Harper wouldn't want his job when he told Kyle's parents.

Hal swallowed and went on with the story. "They said they pulled him up but too late. He was already dead. So, they left him dangling with the rope around his neck and took off, hoping we'd think he hung himself."

Harper held onto Aracella in case she fainted.

Hal turned to Abby. "Phillip. I promised him I'd keep him updated on our progress. This is the first info we could release."

"He's not here, but I'll call his cell Yes, he deserves to know."

"What about Grace? Have you told her?" Madison asked.

"She took the news hard. Didn't want to believe Kyle did that to himself."

"The boys ain't gonna get away Scott free, are they? In my book, they still killed him." Harper had a feeling all along, the news wasn't going to be good.

"No, not entirely. The court will place them in a detention center, but they won't be tried for first-degree murder. They took a plea of guilty to unlawful death." His arm squeezed around Madison. "Do you want me to go with you to tell the kids?"

"Would you? I don't know how Julianne will bear-up under this. I may need you to help with Noah. He may not be able to take her lashing out at him. He needs his father, but I can't risk that. My kids are too vulnerable. Simon would only make it worse." She turned to Abby and Harper. "I have to go to my children."

"You go on. I'll stay for as long as Miss Abby needs me, Chloe will be in soon. She had a meeting with the Child Protective Services this morning." Harper answered, but Madison was already on her way out the door.

Harper put one arm around Abby and the other around Aracella. "We're all family, aren't we? It's good

to have family and help each other. This is the first time I ever felt
like I had real family since my momma died, and I don't remember too much before then.

. "We are family, Harper." Abby kissed the top of Harper's head. "Guess I'd better go upstairs and see if I can locate Phillip. I'll be back to help with lunch."

The circumstances could be better, but at least now, Miss Abby had a reason to contact Mr. Phillip. Maybe something good could come from today after all.

Abby lifted one foot in front of the other as she slowly climbed the stairs to her apartment. She was both agitated and excited over calling Phillip. She needed to prepare herself before speaking to him.

Abby took the phone from her ear, ready to press the off button when she heard the familiar voice answer. "Hello, Phillip Barnes here."

"Phillip, it's Abby."

"Abby, how are you?" Without waiting for an answer, he said, "Have you found out anything on Cynthia?"

"No, that's not why I'm calling. Detective Mainer asked me to let you know they have three boys in custody for killing Kyle."

"Good heavens, tell me about it. Who did it? How are Julianne and Noah?"

"Okay. Give me time and I'll tell you." Even though the circumstances were grim, Abby found it easy to converse with Phillip as she related the news Hal Mainer had given the women at the café. Then a silence stood between them. What should she say now?

"Phillip, have your investigators learned anything about Cynthia or Connie?" She might as well speak what must be on both their minds.

"Nothing much. Nothing except to verify the details you gave me."

"Verify? Didn't you believe me?" She told herself to stop it before they got into a verbal fisticuff. "Sorry, I didn't mean that."

"Abby, it's just that the detectives need to recheck every little detail so we don't overlook anything. Of course, I believed you."

Abby took a glass of water from the refrigerator dispenser. "I'm sorry, Phillip. Lately, I wear my feelings too much on my shirtsleeve. I went to Bowling Green but didn't find out anything." *Anything about Cynthia, that is.* The letters from her mom remained, unopened, in the shopping bag.

"Thank you, Abby."

"Why are you thanking me? She's my daughter, too."

"I know, but you said you didn't want to put yourself out there to be hurt again. That's why I haven't called."

"Well, you got me thinking about finding Cynthia, and I needed some time away, so I took a trip down to the country. Visited some friends and relatives, but no one knew anything at all about Connie, Brian, or Cynthia. Not even the neighbors. This is why I didn't want to begin a search for Cynthia. It hurts too bad to continue butting my head against brick walls."

"I understand. I really do, Abby, but my head doesn't have scars on it yet, because I've only begun butting."

"Phillip, I'll help in any way possible, but I've already tried every avenue I know."

"True, but maybe it's time we skipped the avenues and traveled some dirt roads. They have to be somewhere."

Abby toyed with the phone before answering. "You do realize it has been over forty years. Connie or Brian, maybe both, may have passed on by now."

"That's a possibility. How old were they then?"

"Not sure. I think in their thirties. They'd be at least seventy by now."

"Well, they could still be alive. I'll tell the private investigators to check death records and nursing homes."

"Good idea, Phillip, but if they're good as you say, they've probably already done that."

"Guess you're right, but, Abby, I can't continue sitting around here on my tail and do nothing. There's got to be something I can try."

"I know how you feel. Those thoughts plagued me for years until I realized they had outsmarted me, and I could do nothing. That's when I opened MsFitz Café and began employing single moms who need assistance. At least I can give encouragement to other girls who need the help. Help I didn't get. Guess we all chase our own rainbows."

"And you are so much better off for having done that. Those gals love you. Abby, you call me wealthy, but you are the rich one in this case. I am so proud of you."

"Proud of me? No one has ever been proud of me. Well, no one except my girls." She didn't add how good it felt to hear someone voice those words. She hadn't heard them since her mom and dad stopped saying them.

"Don't be hard on yourself. We should stop butting heads and begin putting our heads together."

"Maybe you're right. I don't know."

"You are a remarkable woman, Abby. I'd say that even if I didn't care about you."

"Phillip, please." Her cheeks put off as much heat as the cordless phone she held against her face.

"You are a beautiful, wonderful, caring person, Abbigail Harris. I'll say this now and won't embarrass you with it again. Thank you for telling me about Kyle. Call me anytime, Abby."

"It was good talking with you, Phillip." She held the phone in her hand and looked at it. When she hung up, she'd be disconnected from Phillip. Maybe forever.

"Abby," "Phillip." They both spoke at once.

"You go first." Phillip said.

"I wish you would," she murmured.

"Abby, can we try just one more time to be friends? I'll be patient with you, I promise. Now what did you want to say?"

Abby was silent for a few seconds. "Abby, are you there?"

"Yes, Phillip, I'm here. I just wanted to say, I'd like that."

"Can we go for dinner tomorrow evening?"

"Aren't you in Chicago?"

"No, I'm still in Kentucky, just not in Shepherdsville. Would you like to go downtown to a nice place?"

"Could we go back to the Varanese? I must admit it isn't exactly as I had it pictured, but I love it. The weather report said it would be raining tomorrow. I would love to see the green waterfall. Guess you know how much I love waterfalls and jazz music."

Phillip laughed. You sound like the enchanted twelve-year-old-Abby I used to know. It would be great, but I doubt they will roll back the roof to let in the rain as cool as it is."

"Yeah, you're probably right. Since it's going to be cool and rainy, why don't we find something local? Cattleman's Roadhouse has good steaks, I hear."

"Cattleman's it is then. Pick you up at the apartment at six tomorrow evening?"

"Sure. See you then." She clicked off the phone, turned, and faced the mirror.

"Don't say it"

I never said a word, but now would be a good time to search the closet. If you are determined to go out with that man who keeps on upsetting you, you might as well look nice. You know he'll look sexy no matter what he wears.

"Oh, you! I prefer you not talk like that. I enjoy his company, not his looks."

Abby went to her closet to see what she could put together to wear tomorrow. Yeah, he was sexy. The shopping bag containing the letters from her parents' home sat on the floor in the corner of her closet. She might as well read just one. She didn't need to read them all, just the one dated first.

"Dear Abigail, your father and I have done much thinking and praying. We are so sorry for the way we reacted. Abby's hands shook. She continued reading. *Yes, we were hurt and disappointed, but we were wrong.* Why had she not seen these letters? She turned the envelope over. Someone had written, return to sender, on the back. Aunt Ruth? Why? She finished the first note. *Please come home and we will help you with the child. We love you,* signed, *Momma and Daddy.*

Abby's hands shook. Her lips trembled. Why would Aunt Ruth do this? She picked up another letter and then another, all containing the same message. Her heart played tic-tac-toe in her chest when she read the next letter.

Dear Daughter, why won't you return my calls or answer our letters. Pip Barnes was here asking about you. I told him what Ruth told me. That you are married now, and I don't even know your married name. We wish you and our grandchild much happiness. I am glad you found someone who loves you and will take care of you and our grandbaby. Please bring the child to see us. We will always love you. Momma and Daddy.

She pulled out another envelope. *Only* Aunt Ruth addressed this one to Momma.

"*Dear Lavinia, why do you continue writing to Abigail? Can't you tell she doesn't want you in her life? If she did, she would answer the letters. She is happily married and doesn't deserve to be hurt by you anymore.*"

Abby looked for the postmark date. She wasn't even married at that time. Aunt Ruth thought she was protecting Abby, but instead she doubled the pain. If she could only have seen just one of these letters, perhaps Cynthia would be with her now. Pip *had* searched for her. If only she had known, but too much time and too much bitterness had built a wall they could never tear down.

The next evening Abby slid open the closet door, pulled out her Ann Taylor slacks and jacket. She didn't face the mirror until she was fully dressed but sat at her vanity and put on her makeup without even a glance at the large dresser mirror. That could wait until she was ready for the final inspection. Now where were her gray pumps?"

She held out the perfume bottle and sprayed a mist of White Diamonds toward herself, careful only the mist surrounded her. Then she had to do it. Abby couldn't leave
the bedroom without the final inspection to make sure her seams lay flat and her hair didn't frizz.

The reflection looked her up and down. *Well I must admit you do look nice, but you should have saved this outfit for the Varanese or somewhere swanky.*

"Cattleman's is good. I like to look nice in my hometown where people know me."

So, you're already planning another date? When are you ever going to stop lying down, so he can wipe his feet on you?

"Phillip is not like that. We both kept secrets and got ourselves into difficult situations. Besides, we're just friends and friends don't hurt each other."

Humph, the image snorted. *Just wait and see how far he runs this time.*

Phillip didn't run, but their relationship was never mentioned. Two friends enjoyed a lovely meal. Abby slept like Sleeping Beauty that night, awaking refreshed and ready to begin the morning. She helped in the kitchen, waited tables, and chatted with customers, until she wasn't refreshed anymore. Finally, the busy morning ended, and she slid into the nearest booth, took off her shoes, and wriggled her toes. Pins and needles pricked her feet with nearly as much agony as her aching back.

Madison pushed a wayward strand of hair behind her ear and plopped down beside her. "We better grab a rest while we got a spare moment. Lunch will hit soon." She squinted her eyes at Abby. "Are you okay? You look tired."

"I am. Guess I'm getting too old to work like this." She thinned her lips into a pink ribbon.

Madison patted the back of Abby's hand. "You will never be old. You're too full of life. Seriously, you've earned the right to enjoy an easier life than this. Do you ever think about retiring?"

"As a matter of fact, I was getting ready to approach you on that subject."

"Me?"

"Yes, you. You're about to earn a degree in business, aren't you? How would you like to manage the MsFitz?"

"I-I don't know. What do you have in mind?"

Abby's jaw line crinkled slightly. "To tell you the truth, I am considering retiring. Life is too short never to find time to relax. I might take a cruise or at least a tour bus and see some places about which I've only read. You don't have to commit now. Just wondered if you'd be interested if I could come up with a plan to generate more money. I realize you'd need a decent salary."

"Well, you've dropped a live one on me. I certainly will consider it." Madison chewed her lips and let her eyes focus on the MsFitz Café sign.

Abby's eyes followed Madison's. She'd miss that sign. "It might be foolish of me to even think about it. I've wracked my brain and can't find a way for the café to net more profits. Thought about staying open more hours, but that would mean hiring extra help. And that would mean spending more money. There's still a pretty hefty sum in the bank from Phillip, but it has been set aside for emergency funds. Don't know if my aching bones is considered an emergency."

"Why don't you ask Mr. Phillip for advice? He's a business owner. Where is he anyway? Don't see much of him around here as we used to. Have you two had another spat?"

The warmth of a blush crawled up her cheeks like a schoolgirl. "No, we have not had a spat. We went out to dinner last night. We decided we got along much better as friends than we do as—as …."

"Lovers?" Madison finished Abby's sentence. "I'd like to see you two as lovebirds, myself."

Heat flushed her face again. "No, not lovers, just more than friends."

"Seriously, Abby, you've listened to all my troubles and bent over backwards to help. I wish you felt free to confide in me. I am a great listener and a good friend. If you ever need to talk…." Her voice trailed off.

"You're right, Madison, and I might take you up on that. I keep too much bottled up. For now, though, let's concentrate on this dinner. Think I will call Phillip and ask his opinion."

Chapter 16

The bell dinged, and the first group of hungry lunch customers came through the door. Harper bounced from the kitchen to take the order. Mary Alice Combs held her new baby, wrapped in a pink blanket. Harper oohed, awed, and cooed. "Sweet little fhlentyn. What's her name? Can I hold her after I get your orders? Just for a minute?"

Mary Alice smiled. "Her name's Penny. You may if she wakes up, but I'd hate to wake her."

"I understand, but I just love little ones." Harper smiled at the sleeping child, took the order, and delivered the food. The baby's eyes fluttered and Harper grinned. Mary Alice handed her the baby. Harper gently wrapped her arms around the little bundle and swayed side to side, hummed a mysterious melody then followed with weird and wonderful lyrics, *Cus-ga dee vur mh-lent-in tloose Kie gus-gee tan ur bor.*

Abby's cheeks creased until her eyelid blinked. She went to the ladies' room and freshened up before waiting the next table. When they seated the last customer, Abby asked Harper, "What did you call that baby?"

"I think her name was Penny, why?"

"No, you called her something else."

"Oh, you mean fymhlentyn?"
"Yes, and that lullaby, where did you hear it?" Abby spoke softly.
"I don't know. I just always called little ones fymhlentyn. Seems like someone used to sing that song a long time ago. Seems like she sang it to me. Some things are just too hard for me to remember. Why do you ask, Miss Abby?"
"It's just a word most people never heard. I wondered where you heard it. I love the melody. I'd like to hear more of it if you can remember."
"I'll try. Maybe Aunt Nellie will know."
"I'd appreciate that, Harper. I really would like to know the origin of that song. Abby nodded to her left. "Betty Whitt at table five is trying to get your attention. Better see what she wants."

Abby remembered calling Cynthia, fymhlentyn, just like the pet name Abby's momma had called her when she was little. She thought the word, fymhlentyn, was a pet name Momma created just for her. That's why she'd continued it with Cynthia. Momma was good at making up tongue twisters, Pig Latin, and kids' word games. That's surely all it was. Wasn't it? She'd have to spend some time Googling fymhlentyn to see if it was a real word.

Abby took out a pen and a pad and jotted down the lyrics. Then she went upstairs to her computer and tracked them down. She had to break it into syllables. *Cus-ga dee vur mh-lent-in tloose Kie gus-gee tan ur bor since s*he had no
idea the spelling or the meaning. Then she found it, an old Welch melody, interpreted says, *Sleep my pretty child, you shall*

sleep until the morning. She thought her momma had made it up. Of course. Momma's ancestors came from Wales. Someone in Harper's family probably came from the Welch linage. What a strange coincidence.

For some reason she didn't tell Harper she'd found the song.

The lunch rush ended, Abby left the clean up to the workers and went to her apartment to rest. She kicked off her shoes, sunk into a pillow and propped her feet on more pillows at the foot of her bed. She would rest a minute and then call Philip. Maybe he could help her think of a way to retire without taking the waitresses' livelihood away from them. She had enough to live on, but not to support the restaurant. She needed to work so she didn't have to pay another worker.

Abby picked up her phone and dialed Phillip's cell. Maybe he could help. Either way, she needed a break, and he probably did, too. "Hello, Phillip, are you still in Kentucky?"

"That you, Abby? Yes, I'm still here. Is something wrong?"

"No, nothing new. I thought if you were free, perhaps we could do something tomorrow."

A pleasant lilt relaxed his voice. "Sure. Dinner and that new play at the Center for the Arts?"

"No, I had something else in mind. Tomorrow is supposed to be pretty and warm. Indian summer, I believe. Wear your jeans and boots. I'll pack lunch and we'll go fishing."

His laughter rumbled through two counties, vibrating her ears through the phone. "Fishing, you say? Then fishing it will be."

As soon as the connection broke, Abby drifted off to sleep, her fingers still wrapped around the phone. Her eyes opened as the first ray of sunshine filtered through the windowpane, hopped out of bed, and donned a pair of faded jeans and a black and gray flannel shirt. She was rooting through a shelf in the top of her closet for a hat when the doorbell rang. She opened the door and bent over with laughter. "Oh, my goodness, it's *Pip!*"

Phillip stood there in a pair of overalls and a flannel shirt with a red bandana tied around his neck. He removed his frayed straw hat but left the twig dangling from between his teeth. His eyes took in her jeans, checked shirt and straw hat. "My twelve-year-old Abby."

Abby couldn't help herself. She ran to him, threw her arms around his neck, and kissed his cheek. "Pip, I've missed you so much. So very much. Welcome home, even if it is
only for the day."

Phillip didn't say a word for a long moment. He just held her, his muscles trembling beneath her touch then drew
in a deep breath and nuzzled the top of her head. "I'll be here for as long as you want me, Abby."

That night Phillip tossed and turned, sleep the furthest thing from his mind. Abby had been in a rare mood today. If only he could locate Cynthia, she might be able to forgive herself and him. He'd forgiven her within hours of learning about the adoption. Could she forgive him for not being there for her, and not believing her when she tried to tell him the truth?

It was his father's fault. Phillip could never excuse that man. He didn't even want to. The man had caused so much pain to him and his mother. And, yes, to Abby and Cynthia, also. If his dad had been a decent husband and a good father, Phillip would never have left Abby. He would've been there to support and take care of her and their baby. He'd once looked up to his father, a tall man, almost a head taller than anyone Phillip had ever seen. A strong man with strong opinions.

It was later, as he grew older; he lost much of that respect. Then one day he lost it all. Phillip had read in the paper about the Ku Klux Klan march down Buckman Street, but he shrugged it off. Then he recognized the horse. The tall man, a head taller than the others rode White Power, the horse he fed and watered every night. Now he knew why some nights the horse wasn't there to eat, and neither was Dad. Phillip had dropped his head, praying none of his friends recognized the white-cloaked tall man, his head hidden under a white hood, riding a white horse.

How could one man cause so much pain?

Phillip had not prayed in a long time. He'd said a few words when asked to lead a prayer at a meeting or ask the blessing upon a meal. However, this night he prayed.

****

After Abby bathed and changed into her pajamas, she sat in front of the vanity mirror to brush her hair. *Abigail, do you know what you're doing?* The lady in the mirror pointed her hairbrush at Abby. *You're letting that man get under your skin again."*

"Maybe. Maybe I am, but some people can just be friends. Phillip and I have been friends for many years. He's the father of my child."

Exactly. What do you consider 'just friends?' Just friends don't produce babies.

"This is insane. We are not starting this mirror stuff again. I'm sleepy. Good night."

Abby turned her back to the mirror and went to bed. She snuggled into her pillow then sat up. "I forgot to ask Pip about helping me with the restaurant," she said aloud, smiled and lay back down. Good enough reason to call him again tomorrow. She looked forward to that.

The next day, Abby asked Phillip to meet her and they discussed the future of MsFitz for hours before she summoned the girls to a meeting. "You, too, Aracella," she called into the kitchen. "This concerns you, also."

Abby put the closed sign in the window, locked the door, and joined the workers gathered around a couple of
front tables.

"What's up?" Chloe asked. Aracella tapped her shoulder. "Shhh, give her a chance and she'll tell you."

Abby touched the bridge of her nose and paused for a second. "I'm not sure where to start, but Phillip and I –

"You and Mr. Phillip's gonna get married. Fly girl!" She drew back her hand with splayed fingers ready to give Abby a high-five.

"No, Harper. Will you just listen? As you know, I'm not getting any younger, and, well, I'm tired." Before the O-mouthed Harper and Chloe could ask more

MsFitZ CAFE

questions, Abby added, "Phillip and I discussed ways you girls could afford to keep the café going if I retired. I thought it only right if I gave you the opportunity to come up with your own suggestions."

Abby placed her elbow on the table, looked at Harper and Chloe. "Why don't you ladies get us something to drink? Better put on some fresh coffee, also. Phillip will be here in a few minutes—has something he wants to pass in front of you."

Before the coffee finished brewing, Abby raced to the café entrance in answer to a peck on the door and let Phillip in. He squeezed Abby in a slight, friendly hug, asked Madison about the children, and inquired of Aracella about her daughter. Phillip, always the considerate gentleman. Abby smiled happy they were friends again.

Harper and Chloe carried trays from the kitchen and passed out coffee, tea, and cokes. All eyes stared at Phillip, who explained he had no financial interest in the café but was helping Abby figure out what to do about retiring.

"I think Abby has something to ask you first." He motioned his hand for her to speak.

"As I said, I'm not sure how to go about this, so Phillip graciously volunteered to help. Anyway, how would you each like to be a joint owner of MsFitz?"

"I don't have any money for something like that. As Granny used to say, I don't have enough to buy a dime if you were selling it for a nickel. Would be nice though," Harper said.

"Same here," Chloe echoed Harper.

"Are you talking about incorporating and making us shareholders? That would finalize my answer to your question yesterday. Yes, I'd love to be the manager."

"That's exactly what we're suggesting. Is everyone in compliance with it?"

"Not exactly sure what you mean, but count me in." Aracella answered next.

"Me, too" Harper and Chloe spoke simultaneously.

Phillip sat in a booth across the aisle and leaned over, crossing his arms on the seat back. "Well then, the next decision is how to make MsFitz bring in enough money to pay for someone to replace Abby."

"Can't nobody take Miss Abby's place," Harper answered quickly.

"That's the truth, Harper, but Abby needs some time to rest and enjoy life. She's struggled since she was seventeen." Phillip answered.

"And I plan to be around. I'll hold on to some stock. The lawyer can work all that out and explain it in detail before we sign legal papers."

"Back to the subject at hand," Phillip commanded in a voice, soft but firm. "Take a few days and think on it. After all, this will be your business. I'll be in Kentucky a few more weeks. We need to put our heads together and come up with a plan. You still have money in the fund, but I'm hoping you won't have to use it all. Every endeavor needs a backup fund. So if you decide to expand, you'll need backing. If you hire help, you will need to net enough profits to pay them."

"Ha, I don't have any money to lose. That's what the lady from the agency harped about today, when she made a home inspection visit."

"Won't the welfare people help you?" Harper asked.

"No, not much. I make enough money, so I don't qualify for government assistance, but not enough to live on with a child," Bitterness spewed through Chloe's words. "I'm sorry. I'll stop raving and get back to the subject."

"Maybe this isn't such a good idea after all. I have a business degree but no experience in the business world." Madison chewed on her pencil. "Not sure I want to be responsible for holding your livelihood in my hands."

"With any employment you accept, the business will depend a great deal on you, Madison. You are a smart, honest woman, and that, my dear is what we need," Abby answered. "I think we are all in mutual agreement, are we not?" She waved to the others who nodded affirmatively.

Phillip spoke up. "I have an idea, but I would need to discuss it with Abby first."

"What is your idea Phillip?" Abby was ready to reject a financial gift. She had told him before; his money made no difference to her. That was not why she'd asked his advice.

He was a successful businessman and a good friend. She respected his opinion as she expected him to respect hers.

"Sell me some stock. Take the money and turn this establishment into a bistro."

"Phillip, we don't accept charity."

"Not charity, Abby. I will get my money back. Phillip J. Barnes doesn't make unwise investments. Look at it like this. More people are becoming health conscious, and would love to get away from fast food, if they had quick healthy food at burger prices."

Abby thought about the suggestion, giving the workers time to study on it. He wasn't offering a loan or a handout. If they incorporated, no one shareholder would lose money. The business would stand good for itself and would make either profits or loss. If she respected his opinion, then she'd have to trust him.

"Sorry, but I don't know what bistro is. I'm afraid I couldn't cook it right." Aracella dropped her head.

"That's all right. Abby can explain the food to you and get you some recipes.

"I'm not an expert, but from what I've learned, they are more inexpensive and consume less time than an upscale restaurant." Abby looked at Phillip for help."

Phillip touched Abby's hand. "Most usually, the bistro is quite simple and serves easily served menus, although that is not always the case. Some are genuinely nice and expensive. We must decide first if this is what we want. As I said, take a few days to think on it. Go on the Internet and look up bistros and any other ideas of which you may think. We could think about catering service, or a specialty restaurant. You also need to discuss among yourselves if you want me as a shareholder.

Abby watched the green sign blink on and off. She loved this place, but she honestly couldn't see it ever growing as it was. The customers were regular and loyal. Nevertheless, there were only so many breakfast and lunch buyers. Several restaurants served home-cooked

meals. "I vote to try for it. But, Phillip, will not give us more money than his shares are worth." She looked at him with
eyes that meant what her mouth said.

"Let them think on it a few days, Abby. Don't want them jumping into something they don't agree with."

"We've already discussed it," Madison said. "We will go with whatever Miss Abby and Mr. Phillip think is best."

"Okay, then, I'll speak with Angie tomorrow. Might as well get the paperwork started." Phillip smiled at Abby. She hoped he wasn't putting too much into this friendship because that's all it was. Just an exceptionally good friendship. She didn't back away when Phillip kissed her softly on the cheek before he left her with her friends.

Chapter 17

The jingle of the bell announced the opening of the café door as soon as Harper unlocked it. Chloe looked at the man who entered, turned white as an uncooked biscuit, and lunged toward him. She made a fist, drew back, and punched him in the nose so hard blood spurted. Before she could make contact again, he grabbed her arms and pushed her against the wall, far enough away her kicking feet missed their aim.

"Let go of me, Troy Haden. 'Let go,' I said."

"Then stop kicking me. I didn't come here to hurt you. Just want to see my son."

"See your son, Troy? Why were you not thinking about your son when you hid that stash of coke under his mattress? Did you think the cops wouldn't suspect a scoundrel like you would endanger his kid? Well they did look, and they took Wally away from me. I was lucky I didn't go to jail. Now I'm almost ready to get him back when you show up." She jerked her arm loose and punched him again.

Abby came in from the kitchen one hand under a towel wrapped around her cell phone, ready to silently speed-dial Detective Mainer. "Who is this man Chloe? Shall I call the police?"

"No need to call anybody, ma'am. Go ahead and tell her Chloe. Tell her I'm your jailbird husband and she'll fire you and kick you out the door sooner than you can blink an eye. Nice people like her don't want anything to do with a wife of a felon." His knuckles turned white where he gripped Chloe's arms.

Abby pushed the speed dial. The phone was on speaker, so Hal could hear. "I know who you are. Just because you're scum doesn't make Chloe scum. She proved that by divorcing you. I suggest you leave before the police get here. Detective Mainer's on his way."

Troy released Chloe, took a step toward the door, and then stopped. Aracella bounced in from the kitchen with a heavy frying pan drawn back over her shoulder. "You heard Miss. Abby. Now, get your rear end out of here before this
pan comes down on that empty head of yours."

He motioned to wave her away." I'm going. I'm going. You're a bunch of crazy women." He pointed his thumb at Harper. "You can put that butcher knife away, too. I'm outta here." Stepping back, he repeated, "You women are plumb crazy. I just want a word with my wife before high tailing it." He made a step toward Chloe and she swung at
him again.

Troy grabbed both her hands. "Whoa there now. I was just leaving. Was just wanting' to say I need to talk to you."

She wriggled her hands attempting to pull them loose.

The bell jingled, and Hal walked into the café. "Let her go." His stern voice demanded the man pay attention. "What's going on here? Chloe, are you alright?" Madison quietly slipped her hand from inside her purse.

Abby's eyes widened. Surely that wasn't steel reflecting from inside that handbag.

Abby had wondered if these ladies could get along without her. Misfits or not; it might take frying pans, fists, butcher knives and a purse, but these girls could take care of themselves. And of each other.

"I'm glad you're here. Arrest this man." Chloe pointed at Troy.

"I told you to take your hands off the lady." Hal's right hand inched under his jacket. A light click said he unfastened the snap on his gun holster.

"Yes mister. And who are you?" Troy didn't move.

"He's the Law. Troy, meet Detective Hal Mainer." Chloe emphasized the word detective and glowered at her ex.

Troy frowned and turned his bloody nose toward the detective. "Stop her from beating up on me and I'll be glad to turn this little hellcat loose."

Hal lifted his brow and turned to the others. "Did he hit her? What did he do to Chloe? Why are her arms bruised?"

"No," Abby said, "I didn't see him hit her, but I was in the kitchen at first."

Harper jumped to Chloe's defense. "She had a good reason, or she wouldn't have jumped on him like that. I mean, he come in the door and she lit into him like a little ole banty rooster. I bet she'd a beat him to a pulp if he didn't hold her back. He must've done something awful to her."

"Harper, Shhh," Abby, shushed her, but Harper was high on excitement. "I just want to tell the detective that Chloe would never act like that without a real good reason."

Hal answered, "I can vouch for her character myself, but because she's a friend to all of us doesn't give her permission to attack someone" He turned to the man standing quietly by the register. "Who are you anyway?"

Chloe answered, "He's my ex-husband. A lousy good for nothing husband and an even worse father. He caused them to take my Wally away. That's who he is."

Hal tapped his fingers on the back of a booth. "Well you two go on now and take your problems with you. I don't want either of you causing any more trouble around here."

Troy turned one side of his lips up into a half-smile. "Now wait just a minute, Detective. Don't I get a say in this? They all seen her. Don't I have the right to press charges or is this little one-horse town like all the others? If you're friends with the law, you can do anything and get by with it."

Hal gripped his hand into a fist but made no offer to hit him. "You have the right to press charges if you want. But let me tell you one thing, I had better not even catch you as much as Jay-walking or you will hear the jail door locking behind you."

"Officer are you threatening me?"

"No, sir, I was not threatening you. I was promising you." He turned to Chloe, "Come on Chloe, let's go down to the station, and work this thing out." He looked at Troy. "And call me Detective."

Abby looked at Hal and could almost read his thoughts. He wished he'd been the one to put that blood on this guy's face.

Chloe turned to Hal, daggers shooting from her eyes. "If you're going to lock me up anyway, let me have another lick at him." She grabbed Aracella's cast iron skillet, but suddenly stopped. She didn't move a muscle except her eyes. "Please, Troy, if you ever loved me or Wally, please don't do this. I can't go to jail. I'll do anything. I hate to beg, but for Wally I'll kiss your feet. I may never get him back if I fail this time. You can't do this to us. Please. I'm sorry. I shouldn't have hit you like that."

"Oh, quit your whining. I'm not pressing charges. Just wanted you to know what it feels like. I don't depend on the courts to get my revenge."

"Thank you," Chloe groveled.

Abby wasn't sure if Chloe was feigning or sincere with her apology. She wasn't sure that crack about revenge wasn't a threat.

Hal turned to Troy. "It's best if you go on and let Chloe settle down. You can call her later if you two have anything to discuss."

Troy rubbed his fingers through his dark brown hair, turned and halted before opening the door. "Chloe, we do need to talk. Call me at Mom's and we can set a time. If you're scared, bring one of your friends with you." He rubbed his nose. "Or maybe I'm the one who needs a bodyguard. Maybe I might have a way to help you get the boy back."

"You do? Could you do that?" Chloe had turned from the hot chick young adult to a chastened, humiliated woman with sagging jaws.

Abby spoke up, "Just go now. Let Chloe get herself together." She wrapped her arms around Chloe. "I'll walk out with him." Hall nodded at Madison. "Be back to get you in a few minutes?"

"Thank you, Hal, for being so understanding. I'd appreciate a second with Chloe."

Hal followed Troy out the door and watched while Abby locked it. Madison pulled Chloe into a motherly hug, "I'd like it if you came home with me tonight. I don't feel comfortable with you going home alone."

"That's a good idea. Or you can stay with me." Abby added.

"Madison, did you have a date with Hal tonight? I don't want to be a bother." Chloe asked.

"No, he was only picking me up because my car was in the shop. You're no bother. We can talk. Or not. Hal will be back in a few minutes."

Abby squeezed Chloe's hand. Do you need to take off from work tomorrow? We'll manage without you."

"No, I'll be better off here." She picked up her purse and jacket." You all have been so sweet to me. I'll tell you everything tomorrow or whenever I can talk about it."

"Whenever you want, we'll be right here, but don't feel obligated to explain anything to me. I have faith in you, girl." The rest of the women nodded in agreement.

"You guys are the best."

They all exchanged hugs and words of encouragement, but neither mentioned the panic in Chloe's eyes.

Jean T Kinsey

Chapter 18

Madison hooked her arm in Chloe's and accompanied her out when Hal pecked on the door, bumping into Philip on the way in. Abby's lips spread into a wide smile. She held the door open and locked it when it closed behind them.

"Abby, Janine said she saw some sort of ruckus over here. Said Hal came in and left again so I didn't presume you needed me. Still, I couldn't go home without checking on you ladies." He smiled and the twinkle in his eyes turned Abby's knees to jelly, yet her face remained stoic. "After all, you might be my next partners in the restaurateur business,"

Abby looked up at Phillip standing a good foot taller than she. "I was going to call you. If you haven't, eaten, what about we go to Cattleman's, and I buy you a steak? I'll tell you all about it there."

"Now that sounds like a good deal since I'm such a pauper I need that money more than you do."

Abby laughed considering what they said in the argument over the ruckus at the bake sale. She poked him in the ribs. "Well, friend, do you think you might spare five for a tip?"

"You girls want dinner? Abby's buying." Phillip grinned at Aracella and Harper.

Harper's eyes gleamed. "Well, I—"

Aracella tugged on Harper's apron. "No thank you. We got plans to go shopping."

"We do?" Harper asked and Aracella tugged again. "Oh, yes. Yes, we do. We'll grab a bite here before we go. It wouldn't look good for our customers to see all of us eating out somewhere else. Might make them wonder about our food."

Abby shook her head, seeing through their ploy. MsFitz served breakfast and lunch. Not dinner. She told them to go ahead and she'd turn off the lights and lock up.

This had been a long day. Abby couldn't help but worry about Chloe. The young woman had come so far. She'd finally told Abby about her past life, how she'd lived a wild lifestyle until she became pregnant with Wally. She quit it all, cold turkey. No more cigarettes, alcohol, or drugs, but she never said why the system had taken her son away until the remark she made to Troy about the stash of cocaine he'd hidden under Wally's mattress. Oh well, Chloe would talk about it when she was ready.

Phillip held the door for her. She handed him the keys to lock up. A good steak and good conversation would take her mind off her girls for a few hours. She needed some rest and entertainment this evening. Phillip always offered her both, proving they could be simply good friends.

Abby filled Phillip in on the previous adventure with Chloe and her ex-husband on the drive to the steak house. "Thank you for going with me, Phillip. I needed to get away for a few hours. I love my girls, but I must admit all the stress is taking a toll on me. I'll be relieved when we get MsFitz changed over to the bistro, and she is supporting herself again, We couldn't have made it this far without your help." She added as they entered the restaurant.

"We could hire more help and then you could rest. Maybe the two of us could take a little trip. Is there somewhere you've always wanted to go?" Phillip caressed the back of her hand with his forefinger, leaving a trace of
tingling sensations behind."

She slowly moved her hand. "I couldn't leave my girls alone while we…" She laughed at herself, remembering how self-sufficient they'd been earlier.

"How would we pay for extra help?" she asked.

Phillip chewed his salad slowly before he answered. "You are taking me on as an investor; we will have the money I invest. You own the building, and the ladies can do the work. If all goes as I predict, we won't need any more mommy fund."

"Do you think so?"

"When you call me Pip, I believe anything is possible. Let's face it Abby, we care about each other. We've never stopped."

"Pip, you agreed," Abby couldn't argue with him tonight. She didn't have the energy. Besides, they'd already settled it. They were just friends. She loved him and always would. If only she'd never given Cynthia away.

"I know I promised, and I will be your friend if that's what you want, Abby. But think hard, if there is nothing left for us, I'll hire someone to oversee my share of the restaurant conversion."

"But what about your promise?" Abby asked. "You promised we would always be friends."

"I know Abby. And I meant it, but I'm a much weaker person than I thought. I just can't do it. I'll keep my promise, but the only way I can be just a friend, Abby, is long distance. I'll always be here if you need me, yet, I cannot see you and be around you without wanting to take you in my arms and hold you. I'm sorry, my love, but I just can't."

Abby didn't answer. She picked up the butter knife, spread the butter on a piece of bread, and nibbled small bits until the waiter brought the steak. The sirloin was tender and perfectly cooked. Done on the outside and barely pink inside, just the way she liked it, but she couldn't swallow the first bite.

Abby was about to choke on Phillip's words. She took a large drink of water. Did she want him to go away? Was she selfish asking him to remain in Kentucky when she couldn't offer him any reason to stay? Those letters proved he had not deserted her. He did come back.

Phillip cut a bite of steak. He looked her deliberately
in the eyes. "Well, what about it, Abigail? Do I stay, or do I go?"

"I thought we had agreed on this." One of Abby's knees hidden under the table shook so hard her shoulder quivered. "Could we ever be happy, or would Cynthia always be between us? You have no way of knowing what I went through alone, and I know how disappointed in me you were when you found I'd given our daughter away. I can't help believing one or both of us would remember the past every time even a trivial argument arose."

Phillip lowered his chin into his fist. "You must stop talking like that. You had no choice for your actions, and neither did I. If we are ever to be happy, both of us must learn to forgive each other and ourselves."

Her lips and chin quivered so hard, she couldn't answer.

They picked at their dinner in silence. So much for the rest and relaxation. Abby lifted her glass of tea, her shaky fingers turned loose, and tea puddled in her lap. Phillip signaled the waiter for the check and asked for a go-box, so Abby could go home and change.

Lines of disappointment spread across Phillip's brow. His lips thinned, pale, and rubbery. If she didn't give him the answer he wanted to hear, he'd probably leave tomorrow. Is that what she wanted? This was not the way she'd planned
this evening.

They drove in silence back to Abby's apartment, gathered the go-boxes, and carried them up the steps. The night was ruined, but that was no reason to ruin good steak. She invited Philip to sit while she changed from her soggy trousers into a lounging robe. Abby didn't really expect him to be there when she returned, but he was. He'd poured them tea and put out plates to finish the meal, which didn't appear as appetizing as it first did. Quiet filled the house. Ear-splitting quiet. Lord, would silence fill the rest of her days?

She touched Phillip's hand, about to tell him she was sorry, but when her lips trembled open, a jumble of different words poured out. Abby had not planned to say, "Don't leave me again, Pip. I need you,"

Phillip's arms gathered her into him before she could blink. "Abby, what are you saying?"

"I'm saying, I have never forgotten about you for one minute of my life. You're definitely right; we can never be just friends. We're not too old, are we Pip? I mean can we have a normal life?"

"We will, Abby. We will." He held her closer, and his lips brushed softly over hers. Abby wilted into his arms.

Phillip murmured in her ear, "Abby, when you say a normal life, exactly what do you mean? I would love to ask you to marry me, but I'm not sure you're ready."

Then ask me. Ask me now. But he didn't. Perhaps it was for the best. "I-I don't know. I just know I don't want to grow old without you. Can we admit to ourselves and the world that we love each other, and then we can take the next step?" That's not exactly what she meant, she should have said, "I'm ready," but she didn't. Patience might be the best way to forge their relationship. *Dear God, let it work this time. I do love this man. I always have.*

"Abby, I love you. I'll spend the rest of my life making up to you for leaving you to face the world alone and expecting my child. Believe me, if I had known, even the Klan could not have chased me out of Kentucky. He put his arms around her again and drew her to him. Their hearts pounded as one. He brushed his moist lips up her throat and moved them over her eyelids. His lips caressed her cheeks. They found her lips, parted and waiting for his. The many years of longing slowly vanished. They stood holding each other, molded into one silhouette until Harper's key turned in the lock. Neither of them moved. After all, they'd agreed to let everyone know how they felt, and for sure, Harper would announce it to the world.

"Oh. Oh my. Should I- I come back?" Harper, eyes big as saucers, usually not at a loss for words, stumbled over every sentence.

"No, Harper, I think Philip will be leaving soon. I have an early shift tomorrow." She did not explain the scene Harper interrupted.

"I think maybe I should spend the night here. From what Abby tells me, I don't trust that Troy guy any further than I can see him. Don't want him breaking in on my two favorite ladies." Phillip sat on the sofa and removed his shoes.

Harper stood with her mouth agape. "Do you want my room, or are you sleeping…" Her cheeks smoldered through her honey taupe skin.

Abby tucked her lips between her teeth, creating a toothless smile.

Phillip laughed aloud. I'll sleep on the couch Harper. I'll be between both my ladies where I can protect them both. His eyes crinkled, and he cast her an impish smile ,then stood, leaned over, and kissed Harper on the cheek. Harper turned her head but peeked around as Phillip quickly kissed Abby on the lips. "Good night, sweetheart."

"Goodnight, Pip."

"Pip?" Harper said, "Who's Pip?"

The next day Abby put a closed for remodeling sign on the door of the café. Phillip placed a call to the construction workers. They gathered all the girls together to explain the café would be closed until the grand opening of the bistro. They would take their vacation pay for the first two weeks and Abby would supplement the rest of the off time from the Mommy Fund.

No one asked the question at first, but plenty giggling was going on as Harper whispered in first one woman's ear and then the other.

Abby simply smiled. Phillip went on in his professional manner until Abby feared the girls might burst from curiosity. Madison cleared the air first. "Okay, Miss Abby. Are you going to tell us, or are we going to drag it out of you?"

Phillip put down his phone and flung his arm around Abby's shoulder. Heat radiated off her face, but she managed to keep smiling. Phillip and I have reconciled some differences which have plagued us since we were teenagers. We are going to try--"

Phillip let out a belly laugh. "Abigail, these are our friends. Tell them we are in love. No formalities needed."

Giggles, ahhs, and handclapping reverberated around the room. Chloe staggered Abby when she asked, "When's the date?"

"So, I guess I need to get my stuff out of the apartment," Harper piped.

"No, you don't need to go anywhere. I thought we'd use this time for some tutoring. Got to get you ready to pass that GED test and then the college entrance exam."

Aracella wrinkled her forehead. "Can I ask a question?"

"Sure, go ahead. What's on your mind?" Phillip answered.

"What is a bistro? I didn't understand before?"

MsFitZ CAFE

"Think I'll let Phillip answer that." Abby laughed. "He's more worldly-wise than us little Bullitt County labor class people."

"You mean rednecks, dontcha?" Chloe chimed in.

"I don't classify my friends, but I'll explain what I've read about bistros on Google. They started in France during the war when the Germans occupied Paris. The Nazi officers demanded food fast, good, and cheap from the small Parisian cafes. Thus, bistros evolved. Sorry I didn't explain it to you more thoroughly before."

"You explained it before, but some of us didn't understand it. I think I get it now. Good, easy, quick and low priced." Harper placed her thumbnail between her teeth and spread her lips into a happy face.

Abby, tickled Harper's ribs. "You got it girl, except nowadays, they aren't necessarily cheap."

Phillip nodded. "You're right, Abby. Some of the upper scale bistros are not so inexpensive or fast now. Many offer a nice dining experience. However, we plan to retain MsFitz in keeping with the original version."

"Now I think I can do it. Mr. Phillip, you make it sound so easy. You said I would need a helper. My daughter graduates from culinary school very soon. I know you try to hire single moms here, but do you think you might consider her? She's earned high grades and knows about all kinds of cuisines—I think that's the word she uses. I could be her helper, instead of her helping me."

Phillip tapped his toes on the floor in silence for a moment before approaching Aracella's proposal. "I won't ask Abby to change her hiring process, but I think this is something we all should discuss since you are now co-owners. At least check her credentials. We need someone who is familiar with the new type of café we're opening."

"I'll go along with that. My policies aren't set in stone and I want the girls already here to get the best from this new movement. I say, let's check her out. Thank you, Aracella. What do you say, partners?" Abby addressed the co-workers.

They all spoke at once making it hard to determine who said what, but all responses expressed agreement. Madison added, "Also, you realize if we can get Isabella straight out of school, her wages will be less costly than someone with years of experience."

Aracella added, "And she's just as good as any of them."

Chapter 19

Harper stopped Madison, Chloe, and Aracella just outside MsFitz Café. "I wish we could do something nice for Miss Abby. She's done so much for us."

"You got something on your mind? Like what?" Chloe asked.

"Well, you know she and Mr. Barnes are going out to celebrate tonight. I wouldn't doubt it if he proposes. I overheard him making reservations at the Varanese for the private dining room. What else would a couple want with a whole room to themselves?"

"Wow, you think so?" Chloe's eyes widened.

"Well, I'm hoping at least." Harper's face lit up. "I sure do wish we could get her a nice outfit to wear. She really doesn't have many clothes. Just that good pants set and the new skirt and blouse. She's worn them both when she's out with him."

"That's a nice gesture, Harper. If we put our heads together, maybe we can think of something." Madison sucked in the insides of her jaw for a moment.

"I know." Aracella said, "Instead of putting our heads together, why don't we put our money together and go shopping?"

Harper suggested the mall, but Madison didn't think they had the time or the money, so she suggested

Cato. "Miss Abby can use a little sprucing up, and Cato has some nice clothes at discounted prices."

"Yeah," Chloe said, "I bet we could each put in twenty bucks and get her all gussied-up head to toe. Can we all afford twenty?"

"That's about what I was thinking," Harper agreed.

"Then let's get going in case we have to return it this afternoon." Aracella hugged herself. "I'm so excited."

"Probably won't have to return anything. I know her sizes." Harper rocked on her toes. "What do you think of the color peach? Seems to be the going trend this year."

"Peach would look good on Miss Abby, "Chloe said.

Her girls had given her the nicest present. Having her employees as friends blessed her daily. Abby turned in front of the mirror.

You don't consider the color too bright for you at your age?

"Of course not. One is only as old as she feels, and right now I feel like putting on this light peach dress with the bright coral-peach-splashed jacket with this lively purse to match." She picked up the purse and waved it at the mirror.

Well I just hope all that color blinds no one.

"If it doesn't, maybe this shrimp nail polish will." She wiggled her painted toes at the mirror. "Went to Walmart and got a pedicure today."

Walmart! Well I never. Are there not any spas in Shepherdsville?

"I probably could have found one, but why? No one can do pedicures like Cao. He's the greatest and he works at Walmart." She lifted her leg and ahhed over the remembrance of Cao's leg massage after he wrapped them in steaming hot towels and his fingers worked the magic on her tired muscles.

"I'm going to have a good time tonight. There's nothing you can do to destroy my self-confidence. I am a woman in love."

Abby turned her back to the mirror as the phone rang. "Hello. Yes, Phillip."

"Uh, Abby, something has come up. I can't talk about it now, but I promise to explain tomorrow."

Is something wrong? Can I do something?"

"No, not exactly. I'll see you tomorrow. Love you."

"I understand. I'll see you then. Love you, too." She tried to disguise her disappointment and said she understood, but she didn't. Something didn't ring true. He'd said he'd see her tomorrow so the emergency couldn't be at the company. Why didn't he tell her if something was wrong in Kentucky? Oh well, Phillip promised to explain tomorrow, and he would. She trusted him.

Abby went to bed early with a good book and was ready for the breakfast crowd bright and early the next morning. Then she remembered. She'd closed MsFitz for remodeling.

Abby picked up her book, thinking of lingering over a cup of coffee and went to Frisch's for breakfast, where the greeter led her to the only empty booth left. As she sat, Abby recognized Janine in the booth behind her, but Janine was talking to her friend, that author, Becky

Kelley. As they sat back to back, while Abby studied the menu, she overheard part of the conversation.

Janine said, "I couldn't believe it was her. I hadn't seen Aunt Miriam since I was a tot. She was frail, thin, and hanging onto Uncle Phillip like a clinging vine. Yet, still almost as beautiful as ever.

Abby left the menu lying and went back to the apartment for coffee. She didn't want breakfast. She'd finish *Heaven's Bait* another day.

Harper had gone to her Aunt's last evening, and the apartment was quiet. Too quiet. Where was Phillip? Why was he with Miriam? Why was it so imperative he had to break their date?

Abby sat out on her deck, overlooking the town. She forced her mind to close down and not think. She learned this trick back when things were nothing but bleak for her. She could bear the loss of her daughter if she didn't think. Didn't feel.

She didn't know how long she sat there numb, but a cold breeze caused her to shudder. She couldn't help but feel the cold. Her mind also came alive. She'd told Phillip she trusted him. He had told her he loved her, and he'd promised to explain today. Did she doubt him? Abby bit her lower lip. "Forgive me, Phillip. I do believe you." She remembered reading a verse from *1 John - There is no fear in love; but perfect love casteth out fear.* She was not afraid to love or trust. She loved Phillip.

When the step boards squeaked from Phillip's footsteps, Abby answered with a smile and a kiss.

"Oh Abby, I have to tell you something, but I was so afraid you'd be upset. Especially when Janine said she saw you leaving Frisch's. She wasn't sure how much you'd heard of her conversation."

"I heard enough."

"You know where I was last night?"

"No, not where you were, but whom you were with, but I believe there was a good reason, and you will explain it to me."

"I was afraid you wouldn't permit me to tell you everything. Let's sit on the deck in the cool morning breeze."

Abby grabbed a sweater and grinned slyly. "At first, I was shocked beyond feeling —dazed. Then I understood with love comes trust and I love you Phillip." She stared into his eyes. "Do you realize I'm still waiting for that explanation? Placidity only goes so far." She half grinned.

Phillip's face flushed. "Again, I'm sorry. Just kick me if you want to."

"I might do that if you don't tell me why you stood me up for another woman." The half-smile turned into a quarter-smile.

Phillip dropped his head and spoke with a voice Abby was not accustomed to hearing – defeat. "Dear sweet Abigail, I'm afraid I'm going to hurt you once again."

"Pip? What is it? Please tell me. Tell me now." Aware Phillip could see the trust leaving her eyes; she still tried to hang on to a remnant of it.

"It's Miriam."

"I know that, but what about her? Are you trying to tell me you and she are—?"

"No, Abby, no. I'm trying to find the words to tell you."

"I've always found the best way is just say it." Abby wanted to kneel and hold on to the floor to keep it from falling from under her.

"Miriam is dying and it's my fault."

"Oh." Now Abby was at a loss for words. "What's wrong with her? What does she want from you?"

"I'm not exactly sure what she wants, but she blames me for her illness. See, when we were first married, I worked day and night trying to get the publishing business on its feet. Barrett Publishing was in trouble and going under. Dexter Barrett offered a full partnership if I could save the company. I did save the company but lost my marriage."

Phillip squeezed his knee, and then rubbed the wrinkles from his pants leg. "She found herself with nothing to do. To kill the boredom, she drank. She wanted children, but I couldn't see bringing a child into a home with the father absent half the time and a mother under the influence of alcohol the other half."

Abby set a cup of coffee in front of him. "Drink this and maybe you'll feel better."

He took a swallow. "She says if she'd had a child to care for, she would never have drunk so much. She blames me for her terminal situation, and deep down, I know it's true. It takes two to make a marriage work and I wasn't there for her."

"You didn't say why she's terminal."

"Alcoholic cardiomyopathy"

"What's that?"

"I asked the same question. When one consumes alcohol over a long period of years, the heart muscle can wear out. Miriam left her disease untreated, and she continued to drink. Now the doctors can't help her. She's in the last stage."

"But that's from her own doing. Sure, you neglected her, but who has not been neglected some time in their life?"

Abby ran her finger over the rough wood of the porch rail. She knew what abandonment was.

Phillip must have seen it in her face. "Yes, sweetheart, you know how it feels to be forsaken, but most are not as strong as you. Some people just fall apart."

And I didn't? I just gave my child away.

Abby had to get control of herself. One moment she blamed Phillip and the next she accused Miriam of bringing it on herself. Then who appointed her judge and jury. Phillip would have to work this out for himself, as she'd had to do.

"Do you want more coffee, Phillip?"

He lifted his cup toward her. "Do you have sweet tea?"

"Sure do. Think I'll have some myself." She took the cup with her left hand, stuck her right forefinger in her mouth, nibbling on a tender spot where she'd rubbed the coarse boards.

The sun had scaled the steeple of First Baptist and the new courthouse while she and Phillip sat on the deck of Abby's apartment. It now began its descent toward the West. Soon it would hide all but its rays behind 44 Hill. They'd

been talking since mid-morning and Abby still didn't understand what Phillip's ex-wife wanted from him and how
it would affect her.

"Come on inside, while I fix us a sandwich to go with the tea. I think Harper has a private stock of cookies hidden around here somewhere."

Phillip lumbered after her. Abby had never seen him
in such a mood. Did he still care more for Miriam than he admitted?

"What exactly does she want you to do?" Abby held the glass under the ice dispenser.

"She wants to move in with me, so I can take care of her."

"Is she destitute?"

"Yes, she is. Doesn't even have health benefits."

"What about Medicare?"

"Miriam is only sixty. She'll get disability, I'm sure, but I hear that takes a long time and a lot of hoop jumping."

"Where is she now?" She should have bitten her tongue and not asked that question. Her gut told her she would not like the answer, and Phillip's countenance predicted his reply.

He tightened his lips as if holding back his words. "She's at my house."

Abby thought she'd prepared for the answer, but a boulder between the eyes wouldn't hurt as much as those four words did. She didn't say anything. What could she say?

"Abby, I didn't mean we were together at my house. Janine's there with her now. I'm at a loss as what to do. I've offered to rent her an apartment and hire a full-time nurse. She gets hysterical and says I don't care that she's dying."

"Do you care, Phillip? I mean do you still have feelings for her?"

"I lived with the woman for ten years. She thinks I'm responsible for her condition. Of course, I have feelings, but sweetheart, they're feelings of guilt." Phillip slushed his remains of tea around the glass.

"Am I bound by some code of gentleman's honor to stay with her until…?"

Abby didn't answer.

Phillip pounded his fist on the table. "What kind of man am I anyway? The woman's over there dying, and I sit here wondering which decision to make—which decision might lose your respect for me."

"Phillip, dear," Abby placed her hand under his chin and lifted his head. "Look at me. You have to do what you think is right. I love you, but I can't tell you what to do. Follow your conscience, and I'll understand."

He pressed his lips to the back of her hand. "I don't deserve you, Abby, but can I ask one more favor of you? I mean, I'll understand if you can't or don't want to."

"What is it? I can't answer if I don't know the question."

"Will you go with me and let me introduce you to Miriam? I want her to know, whatever the outcome of me taking care of her, I'm in love with you and will be for the rest of my life. If you are standing beside me, I think she will take me seriously and realize I'm not making excuses to shirk my duty."

"Phillip, I think you just made your decision when you said shirk your duty. You feel duty bound to be her caretaker. Don't you?"

"Abby, you know me so well. Yes, I think I do. But I still want you to go with me to tell her about us."

"This is incomprehensible. I need to think on it."

"Sure sweetheart." He attempted to pull Abby into his arms, but she backed away.

"Not until this thing is settled. I love you, and I'll wait for you for as long as it takes, but I can't share you."

"I suppose I have to accept that, but I need your support, Abby."

Of course, I'm here for you, and I'll go with you tomorrow."

"I'll pick you up then. 10:30 all right?"

The night was long, and sleep came to Abby in short intervals, yet she was ready when Phillip knocked on her door—ready physically but not emotionally. She predicted today would be longer than last night.

Both Abby and Phillip remained almost silent on the trip to Prospect except for a few pleasantries as, how are you, and it's a beautiful morning. Abby felt awkward, and she supposed Phillip did, also. Why had she taken so long to
admit she loved and needed him? They could have been married by now.

Phillip pulled into the drive of a two story, massive, white house.

"Phillip, this is grand. A real country estate."

"Belonged to my mother's parents. It was a shame she couldn't return to it." His knuckles turned white from gripping the steering wheel. "Come on and let's get this over with."

The lady sitting with Miriam met them with a smile and exited to another room as soon as they came in the door.

"Does she require around the clock care?"

"She brought a nurse with her, but she had some personal things to take care of today. Mrs. Wilson, our housekeeper sits with her sometimes, if we're both gone for a while, in case Miriam needs something from the kitchen. I've installed a monitor, so we can hear from various areas of the house. She prefers not to come out of her room often."

Phillip laughed. "Mrs. Wilson appreciates the monitor. She and Miriam don't get along too well. She listens in case Miriam pages her."

Abby wrinkled her brow.

They continued to a rear bedroom and Phillip knocked on the door. "Miriam, can we come in? There's someone I want you to meet."

A weak yes resonated from behind the bedroom door, and Phillip opened it. "Miriam, this is Abigail Fitzgerald. Abby to her friends." Abby took a small, slender, pale hand.

Phillip stood straight and tall, put his arm around Abby's waist, and said to his ex-wife, "Abby and I are more than good friends. I told you about her yesterday. I say good friends only because she refuses to continue a relationship with me under these circumstances."

Abby swallowed and took a breath. The correct words wouldn't come.

"Hello, Abigail, I'm sorry to meet you *under these circumstances*. She rolled her eyes at Phillip, "but rest assured you won't be forced to wait too long." Miriam smiled.

Abby didn't expect a greeting like that. Another swallow and another breath. "Hello, Miriam, I-I – We're not waiting for anything except your recovery. I surely hope you will soon find a good quality of life."

"Oh, my goodness, Abigail, don't be coy. I know I'm dying. No need to pussyfoot around it."

Phillip stepped between Abby and Miriam. "Miriam, stop it. Abby is only here because I asked her to come. We-I wanted you to realize how much we care for each other and wish you would not put us in this ridiculous position."

"Well, since you don't care enough to grant me this one request, just go ahead and kick me out. I'll live alone what short time I have left."

"Miriam."

"Forgive me, I'm sorry. Didn't mean to whine." She flipped her hair and leaned forward. More cheerfully, she said to Abby, "It was so sweet of you to come and be honest with me. Most women would not. You seem to be a nice person. I'm terribly sorry for causing you pain. Can you please understand why I ask this one last thing of Phillip?"

"As I said, Phillip is a gentleman. I empathize when he accepts his responsibility so profoundly."

"You are kind. Now, please I must get my rest."

MsFitZ CAFE

Abby waited by the doorway while Phillip helped Miriam lie down. "Here's your medic alert necklace and your cell phone. I'll be back in a couple of hours." Miriam reached out and gently touched his cheek. "I'll be all right if you hurry back. You must take Abigail back to Shepherdsville." She smiled sweetly."
"I'll let Mrs. Wilson know I'm leaving." He opened the bedroom door. His cell phone rang, and Phillip answered. "I'll be right there."
His face drained of color. "What's wrong?" Abby asked.
"Joey's been in an accident. Janine's at the hospital with him. It looks bad." He turned to Abby. "You don't know how badly I hate to ask, but I must go. Can you stay here awhile? I'll either come back soon or send a cab for you. Mrs. Wilson's in her work room."
"Phillip, be careful. Can I come with you?"
"Thanks, sweetheart, but I don't know how long I'll be at the hospital. I'll call you as soon as I know anything." He ran to his car and drove away.
Abby couldn't have said no, but she wished she could. She'd just stay with the housekeeper. That's all Phillip asked her to do.
She stepped into a room of sunshine with bright yellow curtains and cushions, situated in a nook off a kitchen that the MsFitz' cook would envy. Abby gave Mrs. Wilson the message from Phillip. The gray-haired, plump, little lady welcomed her and insisted on serving tea and croissants.
Their conversation buzzed along easily. It seemed Mrs. Wilson loved Phillip as much as Abby did.

Protective, too. This, of course, led to the discussion of Miriam. The housekeeper's doubts compared to the ones Abby had attempted to hide.

"There's something strange going on in there." Mrs. Wilson nodded toward Miriam's direction. "I get these bad vibes? What do you think?"

Abby shrugged and took a drink of tea. "Anything I'd say would sound as if it were coming from a jealous girlfriend, but I understand your reservations."

"Reservations. Huh. Try certainties. That woman's been up to no good her entire life. I've worked for Mr. Phillip ever since before she left him. Tried to take every dime the man owned. She got a hefty settlement, too."

"Really, I hear she's destitute now. That's too bad. Alcohol is an evil demon once it gains control of someone's soul."

"I agree there, but one has to have a soul before anything can control it. And if she's destitute, how does she afford a private nurse? Or will Mr. Phillip be stuck with that, also?"

"Oh, I don't know, and don't dare speculate," Abby answered, determined not to gossip, but Mrs. Wilson was making her resolve hard to keep. Abby maneuvered the conversation in another direction. "Do you think we need to check on her, or is the monitor on? *Monitor.* Oh, my goodness can she hear us?" Abby hoped not.

"No, it's only a two way when we turn the control from here. Miriam can also turn it off from her room for privacy."

"She can just turn it off?"

"She thinks she can, but we can override the privacy down here if we need to check on her, or she can turn it on to call us if she wants, and she wants real often

when Mr. Phillip's here. Got a camera too. Not sure if she's aware of that either. See." Mrs. Wilson flipped the control button. Miriam and the nurse sat on the side of the bed, laughing, and
drinking from wine glasses.
    Abby flipped the camera control. "We can't watch that. It's - it's spying."
    "I wasn't spying. Only showing you how to operate the camera. See, simply flip this little switch." She pushed it up.
    Both Abby and Mrs. Wilson gasped. The nurse and Miriam stood by a raised window fanning smoke from their cigarettes out of the room and sipping from their wine glasses.
    Abby didn't insist on turning the camera off. Her eyes searched for the oxygen line running from the closet. The tube lay on the table by the bed. She'd seen enough. Abby told the housekeeper to turn off the camera.
    "She's not even sick, is she? Phillip should know about this, but how can we tell him?" The dimple in Abby's cheek inflamed.
    "Just tell him what we saw."
    "There must be another way." Abby's lips converged into a thin pink line. "I don't want Phillip to think I don't trust him and would stoop to eavesdropping. We've had trust issues in the past and I can't chance that again." She didn't doubt Phillip, but she, for sure, questioned Miriam. What was that woman contemplating?
    "I guess you know I don't like Miriam, but that has nothing to do with it. We both love Mr. Phillip and

don't want her taking advantage of him. I think in that fancy-pancy head of hers lies a devilish plan. We have to warn him, but he'll fire me if he believes I was spying, and I need this job."

Mrs. Wilson sat quietly for a while, biting her lips, then looked up at Abby. "You know, if I expect Mr. Phillip to believe me, then I gotta trust him, too. I'm going to tell him."

Abby darted her eyes to her empty ring finger. "You're absolutely right. We'll do it together."

"You'll do what together? Are my two ladies cooking up an elusive plot?" Phillip had entered the room.

"Well, ah, Mr. Phillip, I was just ah showing Miss Abby how the monitor works and ah…"

"I'll tell him, Mrs. Wilson." Abby repeated to Phillip the monitor's expose'. "Phillip, we were not snooping on your ex-wife. I hope you know that. Neither Mrs. Wilson nor I."

"Of course. I'd believe anything either of you two ladies told me. I hope you believe that. But are you certai you didn't misinterpret? Could you have misunderstood?"

"We saw it clearly, Phillip. She had her oxygen off, standing, walking, smoking cigarettes, and drinking wine. If you doubt—"

"No Abby, I don't doubt either of you." Phillip pulled Abby into his arms and nudged Mrs. Wilson. ""Do you know what this means? Abby, we are free. Wouldn't have bothered me one bit if you two were snooping. Marry me. Marry me, Abby, before anything else can keep us apart." He spun her around, but instead of answering she asked, "But what about Miriam?"

"Miriam can answer to my lawyers. I don't even want to listen to more of her lies. Come on beautiful ladies, I'm taking you out to eat in the finest restaurant in town. Let's
lock up the house and let her wonder why no one answers the monitor."

The two wide-eyed women blinked eyelids at each other. "Yes" they said in unison.

"In fact," Phillip added, "I'm pampering my finest ladies to a Hilton suite near here, and you, my comrade and housekeeper, may invite a friend over to spend a few nights while I take Abby home and then see my attorneys. Hey, we got three beds. Invite three friends." He squeezed the ladies' shoulders into a big hug.

After they settled in the three-room suite in the East End, Mrs. Wilson pulled the drapes. "What will she eat? I didn't prepare her a thing."

Phillip ordered coffee from room service, and impertinence twinkled from his eyes. "Frankly dear, in the words of a wily gentleman, I don't give a damn."

*****

Abby and Phillip followed the rising sun cross-country from eastern Jefferson County toward northwestern Bullitt. Conversation was easy. Phillip responded in his usual carefree way, free of burden the same, cumbersome burden as she. He picked up her hand and kissed her fingers. "Sorry I missed that date at the Varanese, but if you are free, I've reserved that little private dining room for tomorrow night. Wear something pretty." His lop-sided grin dug into her heart.

"I will. I have a real peachy outfit ready to go, courtesy of my girls. Did I tell you I love you Phillip Barnes?"

"You did, and you more than proved it yesterday, but I'll never tire of you repeating it."

They pulled into MsFitz drive. "I can't come in. Need to get home and discuss with my attorney about this mess with Miriam. I assume she and her phony nurse are gone by now, but they could be stealing me blind."

"I can't believe you just left. Not even confronting them."

"Truthfully, I was so happy, I might would have let
her off leniently. This way, she doesn't know what's hitting her."

"Phillip, I don't think she has any medical issues; do you?"

"She has issues alright, but self-imposed ones."

"No need to go up. I can see myself in. But promise
me you won't stand me up tomorrow night. I am looking forward to that dinner. And you'll have to come up with a Bonafede, documented, and sealed excuse if you stand me up this time."

He kissed her on the lips. "I promise."

Abby wiggled her ring finger as she climbed the stairs to her apartment.

Chapter 20

Abby turned before the mirror and started the conversation with the image, "Guess Pip will prove you wrong tonight, when I come home wearing his ring." She laughed and circled the third finger on her left hand with two from the other hand. Then she placed them, like a mask over the eyes of her mirror image.

Abby continued laughing as she answered the phone. It was Phillip.

He couldn't make their date again tonight. There was an emergency. The company jet was picking him up in an hour. He would explain it all when he returned. Abby didn't dare peek at that mirror. She told him she understood emergencies came with the profession of owning a large company. However, she didn't understand.

If he had to go to the office, then he had to go. It must be a real emergency if the company jet was picking him up at the airport. Yet, Phillip didn't seem too down in spirits over leaving. In fact, he didn't even apologize.

Oh, well, she'd grab a book and catch up on her reading. Abby searched the bookshelf for a while before settling on *Heaven's Bait*. This new book, written by the local author, Diane Theiler, seemed like it might be a good read once she had the opportunity to delve into it. Abby liked to support local artists.

Abby turned down the simple, hand-stitched quilt she'd purchased from Barbara Hale, a lady she'd met at the quilting club. Simple, but beautiful with tiny little stitches all done by hand--something Abby had never mastered. She changed into her pajamas and snuggled in with the book. Unsure how long she'd been reading or what time it was, Abby tore herself away to answer the phone. Maybe Phillip had changed his mind. They could still have coffee or something. She missed him already and he'd only been gone a few hours.

However, it wasn't Phillip. A woman's voice quivered from the headset, "Ms. Abigail Fitzgerald?" Abby didn't want to answer. She froze. Something was wrong.

"Yes, this is Abigail Fitzgerald."

A sob came through the receiver before the voice. "Oh Miss Abby, something terrible has happened."

"Who is this? What's happened?" Abby collapsed in the chair by her bed.

The voice answered, "This is Janine, Uncle Philip's niece." She stopped for a brief second and then went on. "The plane has gone down somewhere in the Smokies. The pilot radioed they were having engine trouble and then they went off radar. The weather is bad. It's snowing in the mountains.
A search team will be sent out in the morning, but..."

*****

"Mr. Barnes, we got trouble." The pilot told Phillip.

"What is it Harry?" Phillip put his magazine aside and looked toward the cockpit.

"The engines are stalling. Gauges say we're out of gas, but we can't be. Fueled her up before we left Chicago." Harry pecked on the controls.

"What can we do? Should we bail out?" Phillip's stomach folded inwardly, but he tried to remain calm on the outside as he buckled his seat belt. Not now. We got a few minutes left yet. The first engine sputtered out a bit ago. I turned and headed down the mountainside. The nearer the bottom, the easier we'll be found."

They were really going to crash. If only he could say what was in his heart to Abby. Why had he not formally proposed? Abby wasn't the kind of woman who expected fancy restaurants and big diamonds. She never was. All she expected was unconditional love.

The pilot was speaking to him. "We are over a heavily wooded range. If I cut the engines now and attempt to glide down into the large treetops, we might make it." The last engine sputtered. "Treetops should break our speed. Might have a chance."

"Do whatever, but radio for help." Phillip's eyes glued to his steepled fingers. "Tell them we're going down."

"Already did that, sir. They'll find us." Phillip closed his eyes and prayed as the plane bounced over treetops, jerked some up by the roots, but as the pilot predicted, dropped in speed as it went. Then it crashed.

*****

Abby had not said a word since she answered the phone. She arose from the chair by her bed and held the phone. Unable to say anything. She heard Phillip's niece speak the words, but she couldn't comprehend them.

"Miss Abby are you there?" Janine's voice trilled through the phone "Miss Abby?"

Abigail opened her mouth, but words wouldn't come. Her throat choked. Abby opened her mouth and closed it again. Only a whimpering moan emanated.

"Miss Abby, please, are you, all right?" Janine questioned.

She finally exhaled an answer, "Yes," before she dropped the phone and crumpled across the bed. *Dear God, please find him and bring him home to me.* Sobs raked her body. Harper heard them from her bedroom and came
running. Between sniffles and wails, Abby finally told Harper about the plane crash.

Harper hugged her, patted her, wiped her forehead back to the hairline, but cried almost as much as Abby. "I'm calling the other girls. They need to know."

"It's so late, don't bother them."

"Miss Abby, they're family." Harper dialed the phone.

In less than ten minutes, Abby's implemented family was there. They made her tea. She wasn't sure if she drank it. Madison coaxed her to stop crying; she shouldn't be sick when Mr. Phillip came home.

Abby sat up and dried her eyes. "Janine." she said. "She doesn't have a living soul to comfort her, and Phillip was like a father to her. She picked up the phone and insisted Janine come over. The café sisters left the two broken women and Harper in the living room to comfort each other while
they went to Abby's kitchen to make snacks and coffee.

"Here, try some warm cookies." Madison passed the cookie plate while Chloe and Aracella brought in the coffee carafe and lemonade. Harper didn't budge from Abby's side.

Abby, somewhat in control of herself by this time, wiped her swollen eyes and blew her nose before she accepted a cookie and coffee. Comforting Janine helped her to help herself. Yet her knees still trembled so her legs shook her pajamas.

"Thank you, sweeties, but you don't have to stay here." She looked at Madison. "Who's with your kids?"

Madison smiled. They are fifteen and seventeen. Old enough to stay home alone. We're here because we want to be. Janine has her cell phone with her. We want to be with you when the call comes saying they found him."

Abby patted the sofa cushion beside her. "Come sit down then. I have something to tell you. This is all my fault and I need to tell someone. I've held it in too long. After what I did, God will never let me be happy." She entwined her fingers bending them backward, until two of them popped. "I should have known."

Harper, eyes red from crying, tugged at her shorty pajamas and let out her breath. "Miss Abby, what are you saying? You'd never do anything that bad. You're the best person I know."

Abby insisted the girls listen because she only had the courage to say it once. She wished Phillip were here to help her, but he was gone. Not knowing what the next few days might hold, their secret needed to come out. "I'm not that good, Harper. Why do you think I've been working so hard, but to pay for my past?"

"You don't have to explain anything to us," Madison said. Aracella and Chloe agreed. Harper sat wide-eyed.

Abby spoke in her slow, monotone voice--almost tranquil, although she was far from calm inside. She told them about the night at the river, Cynthia. Everything. "But that's not the worst of it. I tried. God knows I did, but I couldn't work and take care of a baby. Not on a waitress' salary and pay a sitter." I was barely eighteen and no high school diploma. Then she told them she gave away Phillip's and her little girl. She had no right to happiness, and God knew it. "I struggled to make up for my transgressions by helping other single moms. That's why I try to employ young ladies with children, take them under my wing, and play mother hen. I try to assuage the pain I feel, but I can never make up for what I did. This is my punishment."

Chloe jumped from her seat, placed her hands-on Abby's shoulders, and gently shook her. "Butter my biscuits, Miss Abby. What is it you told me? You said if I repented for my wrongdoings, God would never remember them again. I was beginning to believe you. Does God have a different set of rules for you than for me?"

"She's right, Abigail. You spoke those words to all of us many times." Madison agreed. Abby sat with her elbow resting on the table, chin resting on her palm, chewing on her little fingernail.

"Miss Abby, look at it like this. Those people loved your little girl, or they wouldn't have taken her away like that. At least she knew she was wanted. Some people don't ever have that." Harper bit her bottom lip until it stopped trembling. "After my mom and daddy's car wreck, nobody ever wanted me again. I feel more loved right here than anywhere else. Almost feels like real family. You all don't care about the color of my skin. Some folks around here think white is good. Others say black is fine, but few think half-black and half-white is anything. You just think of me as Harper."

Abby bowed her head in silence for a moment. "Thank you, girls, for getting me back on track." She added, "I'm sorry," perhaps more to God than to her friends. Everyone dabbed their eyes at unabashed tears. Some for Abby and Harper, the rest for Mr. Phillip.

Abby's little family surrounded her. She reached for Harper's hand. "Let's pray for Phillip. He's gotta return home."

She dropped to her knees by the sofa. They all joined hands and bowed there in the living room, each saying their separate prayer but in unanimity as one. Phillip would come home. No matter how the odds stacked against him, he would come

*****

Phillip's head pounded. His body, one big ache. What had happened? He looked through the window and remembered. "Harry. Harry! Where are you?" he yelled into the empty cockpit. Had they been here all night? The morning sun peeped over the eastern mountaintops.

Phillip's door wedged tight against a tree. He couldn't budge it. A strange noise, oink, snort, oink came from below the plane, and Harry was missing. The cockpit door hung by one hinge. He made his way from his private seating to the cockpit.

Phillip jumped to the ground. "What in the world! Get off him. Get, I say!" He waved his arms, kicked, and shouted. A wild boar was attacking unconscious Harry. Phillip grabbed a jacket and waved it in the boar's face. Hogs were not supposed to attack humans, but this one found Harry on the ground and didn't want to give up his dinner. The boar aimed for one last bite before backing off. Pain brought Phillip to his knees. That one last bite left tooth slashes in his leg. Now what should he do? They both were bleeding, and Harry was comatose. Phillip knew little about wild boars. Did they run off into the woods when frightened, or did they come back for their prey?

*****

Neither Abby, her girls, nor Janine expected sleep that night, but the shock left them tired. They fell asleep, one at a time until the chairs, the sofa, and wherever they rested filled with sleeping women.

Morning sunrays peeped through the windows of the apartment over the cafe. Abby sat up and rubbed her eyes, her faced filled with a quizzical frown. Why was she curled up on the couch? Her eyes roamed the room and rested on Janine, leaning back in the recliner. *Oh my God.* She remembered. *Pip.* No one called last night. They had not found him.

Running her hands through her messed-up hair, she answered the tap on the door, Harper and Aracella, on her heels. Janine sat up but didn't speak. Madison still dozed. Hal Mainer stood in the doorway his arms full of bags of hot donuts from that delicious little Oriental donut shop just
across the tracks. Harper took the bags from Hal who held out his arms for Abby and folded her into his broad

shoulders. "Thought I'd find all of you here. I'm so sorry, Miss Abby. The news came across our police radio this morning. I called my friend Detective Bradley Owens in Knoxville. He's promised to keep me updated at every change."

"Each change? I don't even know what the present is. Only know Phillip's plane crashed somewhere in the Smokies. Can you tell me anything else, Hal?"

"Not much. The pilot was found inside the plane." His eyes drifted to Madison, shaking her head awake on the sofa.

Aracella handed them each coffee.

"Where is Phillip? Did they find him?" Abby, afraid to hear the answer, squeezed her fingers, trying not to wring her hands.

"No, Miss Abby, they didn't find him." The muscles in the detective's throat rippled as his gaze dropped below her puffy eye-level.

The detective's body language, not lost on Abby, signaled concern. "Hal Mainer, you're not telling me something. I see it in your expression. Tell me. Is Phillip dead?"

"I don't know, Miss Abby, and that is the truth." He hesitated, shifted his feet, and continued. "The pilot's barely alive. Some kind of wild animal had chewed on him."

"Oh-my-God." Abby whispered through clenched teeth and grabbed her chest with both hands. "I thought bears hibernated in the winter."

Park rangers are not saying what kind of animal." Looks like Phillip was injured, but he still left footprints, so we know he didn't die in the crash. As far as we know, Phillip is still alive. Nothing about locating Phillip, or any evidence of another wild animal attack."

"It couldn't be a bear. It couldn't. They hibernate."

"I think they sleep lighter in milder climates like Tennessee. A loud noise could wake them." Someone said.

"A loud noise like a plane crash?" Abby wrung her hands.

Hal continued softly. "They didn't mention bears. Don't worry about what you don't know." Sympathy filled Hal's countenance. "They found a set of footsteps, presumably Phillip's, coming from the cockpit and leading away from the crash site. The tracks showed he was dragging his right leg.

"Lots of blood and bandaging in the cockpit. Looks like Phillip pulled Harry Morrison, the pilot to safety, bandaged both Harry and him then went for help. Search and rescue couldn't trail his tracks after he reached the top of the ravine due to the heavy snowfall. And that's all I know." His voice caught in his throat, and he wiped his eyes with the inside of his shirtsleeve.

"I don't understand. Why would Phillip leave the safety of the plane?"

"I was told if he hadn't, they would both have died. The plane had dropped into a canyon. Rescuers couldn't see them, and the massive trees captured the flares. They said Phillip tore strips of clothing and any material handy and marked the trail down to the plane. A pilot spotted a piece of red material flying from a tree branch. Search lights followed the descending trail and found the comatose pilot."

"I'm going."

"You're going where, Miss Abby?" Madison asked.

"I'm going to find Phillip."

Hal reached his arms out and stopped her before she headed for her bedroom and gathered her into a bear hug. She dropped her head on his shoulder and cried.

"Miss Abby," Hal patted her back, "Search and rescue is doing all that's possible to find him. All we can do is wait."

"And pray" Madison added.

Chapter 21

Phillip dragged his leg over the frozen snow while he dug in with the other foot, pulled himself upward, clawed the hardened snow with his hands and hugged onto the smaller trees, and after several hours, made it to the top of the ravine. His irate leg ached and begged him to let it rest, but Phillip couldn't. If he stopped, he would not have the strength to get up. He'd marked a trail and built a fire in hopes the rescuers might find Harry.

Yet, they might not. Over-lapped trees hid the narrow ravine. He needed to continue on. His whole body begged for a respite, but that was not doable. Soon the fire he left would burn low and he only had enough dry wood to keep it going for a short while, especially after he took enough with him in case he couldn't find more. He needed to continue on. Help could be out there somewhere. He must continue on.

He needed to find food, then he'd search for a safe place to rest. In every direction, he saw nothing but snow. No caves, not even a hollowed-out tree uninhabited by a sleeping bear. But wait, he heard something. Running water. Unfrozen water meant a spring emptied into a stream, keeping it flowing enough not to freeze. He'd find it. Might have some fish in it. Hope. How pleasing. Hope.

Just over the next hill, a brook ruffled its way around the terrain. The surrounding scenery– such a beautiful place. Snow-capped mountains as far as his eyes could see. A cloud hung from the top of one of the highest peaks, taking on the form of Abby's face. The scenery so beautiful. A spring-fed stream, clear as precious stones, whispered through the white-carpeted landscape. Abby's face stared down on it.

If only he could touch Abby. Phillip shook himself to regain his senses and vanished the idea quickly. He thanked God he'd kept his trip a secret from her. At least she was safe.

He searched through the backpack for something he could rig into a fishing pole but stopped at the far-off sound. In the distance. A low growl and then a loud howl. Wolves. What now?

The howls came closer. Could they smell the blood on his leg? Darkness would be upon him before he could return
to the plane or find shelter. He couldn't give up. He needed to do something. He must do something. However, what?

Tired, hungry, and frightened, his senses played tricks with his mind. Phillip laughed aloud. If time flies when
you're having fun, he wondered what the cliché was for time flying when you're fighting to save your life.

Phillip still carried a lighter and a small amount of fuel from the plane, but how long could a small fire keep away a hungry pack of wolves? Even if his leg allowed him

to climb a tree, he would freeze during the night. He didn't have time to seek shelter. He put the fluid and lighter away. What good would a fire do him? Prolong the hungry wolf
pack for maybe a half-hour? Perhaps he could light one stick at a time and wave it at them. Might give him about fifteen minutes more this way. Phillip would fight for fifteen more minutes of life thinking of Abby.

*****

Harper sat at the table drinking a Coke, not saying a word. Then she disappeared. Abby supposed she became sleepy and went to lie down. That girl could sleep through a tornado.

Abby searched though her purse to find a card. Who but Phillip's company could afford to help her? She requested a helicopter and a pilot. His secretary promised the helicopter would be on the landing pad within two hours, manned by a pilot trained in search and rescue.

Abby hurried up to her apartment to pack her bag. Two bags sat by the door packed and ready. "How sweet of you, dear, but I don't need this much. Just warm clothing for the mountains."

"I know, Miss Abby. That one's mine." Harper's bottom lip quivered. "You don't think I'm gonna let the only family I can remember go away without me. You or Mr. Phillip might need me for something."

"Of course, I need you. I need you to be right here waiting when I bring him home."

"Miss Abby, if you don't let me go with you, I'll get on a commercial plane and be there right behind you. Might as well go together."

"Harper, what am I going to do with you?" She pulled her young friend into her arms. "Then empty these bags and leave everything you can't stuff into one. Take heavy coveralls for both of us. You do have some?"

"Yep. Sure do. I'm a Kentucky girl."

"Then you better hurry, the company's sending a car out to get us. We'll meet the pilot at the airfield." She turned her head around. "And boots. Don't forget warm boots."

It might take a while to find Phillip, and then God only knows in what condition he could be. A friend on this trip might be a blessing, and Harper truly was a blessing.

Abby would find Phillip. Alive, she prayed.

*****

An adage of his Gramps floated through Phillip's mind. *When on earth, danger surrounds you, look up.* He leaned his head back and gazed toward heaven. The solution stood before him when he raised his eyes upward. Almost covered with snow, a hunter's blind attached to a massive
tree, appeared in front of him. Thin, steel support legs promised it would hold him and the tent. Wolves didn't climb. If he could pull himself up the stand, he'd be safe tonight.

Yet darkness approached faster than the wolves traveled toward him. It was time to build the fire. Why had it taken so long to reach the top of the gorge? Did he

spend too much time at the brook? Phillip promised Harry he'd be back, but he couldn't make it in the dark. He yelled into the cold mountain air, "Tomorrow, Harry.. Tomorrow I'll keep that promise. Hang on H-a-r-r-y! We'll get out, I promise." He
was glad Harry couldn't hear that promise for Phillip always kept his promise. Always before.

    A fire built with the bit of dry wood kindling from his stuffed backpack would keep the wild animals away for a while. He closed his eyes and breathed deeply, enjoying the touch of warmth through his frozen clothing, but he needed to find a way up to the blind before the fire died and the wolves' craving for food led them to brave the embers and come for him.

    He tried, and tried, and tried, but his throbbing leg refused to climb the tree to the hunter's tree tent. Phillip refused to surrender to despondency. He would hold on. Please God help him hang on. He rubbed the leg above the wound. He didn't know what he thought rubbing would do, but he was ready to try anything. It did nothing.

    Again, Phillip's gaze trailed up the steel frame. A snow-painted, handmade rope-ladder, almost hidden in the snowy mist, hung from the hunter's lookout. A rope dangled just low enough he could stretch his frame and arm to reach it. He pulled the rope, and the ladder came down.

    The wounded leg protested as Phillip hefted it with one hand from first one rope-rung to the next, until he fell panting into the tent. He gritted his teeth in pain, yet his eyes widened when he stared at the inside of the tarpaulin shelter. Supplies. Some still in grocery bags lined one side. The hunter must have brought supplies and left when the storm threatened to trap him.

MsFitZ CAFE

Soon the night would wipe out the sun's last ray. Phillip needed to get busy. He tore open bags of supplies: cans of various food, bread, and other camping staples. He found coffee, bottled water, although frozen, and candles without opening all the bags. When his scrutiny spotted a butane camp stove, Phillip lifted his eyes and heart toward heaven in appreciation. Maybe he could go back to Harry after all. Harry, I'm sorry I'm not capable of getting some of these luxuries to you tonight. Phillip laughed above the pain. A camp stove, a can of pork and beans, luxury? This evening they were. And coffee, a real bonus.

He lit the stove, and for the first time all day, he had hope of tomorrow. Phillip sat on a stool to rest, took off his boots and coveralls, and sighed with a deep breath. Yep, tomorrow could be a brighter day. Weak and exhausted, he certainly hoped so. However, the food tonight tasted good.

He gazed back at the boxes. Surely, a haven such as this would have a first-aid kit. And it did. With his pants leg rolled up to his thigh, he examined the upper calf. He was in trouble. The bandage, wet and dingy yellow from pus,
smelled like rotten meat. Phillip removed the sticky bandage. Runny discharge oozed from the open gash he'd taped closed this morning. Hope dwindled away.
Dwindled both for him and for Harry.

Phillip imagined pathogenic parasites clinging to the wild boar's tusks from eating the remains of larger animals' kill. His wound was infected. By tomorrow, gangrene or sepsis could be set in. If they found him soon, he still might lose his leg. If not soon, he'd lose his life.

Exhaustion from his wound and from physical exertion took over Phillip's will power. He had no more fight left in him. He began to shake with chills. The little camp stove which warmed him earlier, didn't prevent the cold from taking over his body. Was it really this cold, or was it chills from fever? His weak hands shook as he fumbled inside the first-aid kit to find a thermometer. It took all the strength he could muster just to lift his hand to his mouth and hold on to the thermometer. He had to stay awake. He must. His temp read out at 104 degrees. It took a minute of rest before he crawled and dragged his leg to the partially thawed bottled water, poured it on a cloth, and held it to his face. He had no more strength.

Abby's face appeared before him but vanished. Appeared again, tried to say something, vanished again. With weak fingers, he pulled her picture from his wallet and dropped it on his chest. When they found him, he hoped they would tell her she was the last thing he thought of before…

Chapter 22

"Ms. Fitzgerald, it pains me to say this, but it might be time to give up. We've covered every treetop in a twenty-mile radius of the constants the other pilot reported. No healthy person could walk more in this weather, let alone someone with a bum leg."

Tears traced a pattern down Abby's cheeks. He was right. Her mind told her so, but her heart refused to accept it. "Can we look just one more day? I told you to call me Abby. Every one of my friends calls me Abby."

"And please call me Ken." He hesitated. "Abby," the young pilot hired by Barnes Publishing said, "The local helicopters have been called in. The ground crew's still out, but they've down-sized to a recovery mission."

Abby wiped her eyes and struggled to hold back her emotions. Recover Phillip's body? No, he was alive, and she'd find him. "I heard that on the news, but I'd like to take the plane out one more time. If we don't see any signs of him, I'll try to accept the worst."

"Alright, Abby, we'll go out bright and early tomorrow."

They were out at dawn and still nothing. "Looks like all is quiet out here. Sure, is pretty if it weren't so sad." Harper peered through her binoculars at the mountain range below.

"It'll soon be time to turn in." The pilot swung the plane toward a sparser stand of trees. I am sorry ladies. I never had the pleasure of meeting Mr. Barnes, but everyone at the company says he's a heck of a nice man.

"What's that?" Harper pointed toward the ground.

"What's what?" Abby careened her neck in the direction Harper pointed and adjusted the lenses on her binoculars. "I see something." She tugged on the pilot's arm.

He cut the throttle and the plane stood still in the air. "Yes, ladies, I believe we do see something, but what?"

"Looks like something red flying through the trees. Can't see it but just now and then, the way it zigzags through the forest. The next thinning of the woods, I'll see if I can get a bit lower."

The red continued down the mountain. At one point, Ken dropped low enough to see the red thing was a flag. Looked like it was on some kind of tall metal post. Some letters on it. Could be SOS. The helicopter followed it.

Ken radioed the airport and identified the copter. "We've spotted a red flag flying through the trees but can't
see to what it's attached. Looks like SOS on a high-flying flag. He gave the location and paid close attention to the dispatcher.

"Follow that flag. It's old Mountain Man Jax. He's a hermit living up there in the mountains. Never comes down but once a year to sell his furs and buy supplies unless." He paused "unless he has found a lost person up there. He's rescued or recovered more missing people in those mountains than all our rescue squads."

Harper spoke slowly as if scared to put her thoughts into words, afraid they wouldn't be real. "Miss Abby, could it be him?"

Ken said he had not heard of any other missing persons in the Smokies.

"Then I'm going to believe it's Mr. Phillip. I prayed all night."

Abby stayed silent. Sometimes that Jax man recovered instead of rescuing.

Ken relayed to the ladies what else the dispatcher said. He recognized the latitude and longitude constants. "Kill Bear Trail. If Jax put out an SOS, he has someone on that little wagon behind his snow mobile. It wouldn't be the first time. He said that giant mountain man knows the trail like the palm of his hand and knows how to dodge the small trees, which has grown since the trail closed." The dispatcher was sending an ambulance to meet them at the bottom of the snow-covered Kill Bear Trail.

"Kill Bear Trail? Wonder where it got that name?" Harper asked.

"Well I'm not from around here, so I don't know for sure, but some of the guys were talking last night at the café around the corner from our motel. One of them mentioned it as being an old Indian trail. They traveled it to kill bear for the winter meat and hides. Sounds logical to me."

"I thought it was a hiking trail." Abby joined the conversation.

"No, ma'am. An Indian trail, or so they say. It wouldn't take us long to follow a hiking trail. Tennessee closed it off because visitors violated the stay out danger-signs. Some of them were attacked by bears."

"Attacked by bears? What about Mr. Phillip and the mountain guy? Are they in danger?"

Abby swallowed.

"No, miss, I heard that mountain man, Jax, could kill a bear with one hand. That's what I heard." He smiled at Harper. "According to my calculations, we should get there in another half-hour or forty-five minutes." He swept his eyes over Harper behind him and Abby in front with him. "Now you ladies be prepared for anything. Hopefully, it will be

213

good news, but one never knows."

"Anything?"

"Yes, Harper, anything." Abby picked up Harper's hand and squeezed. "It might not even be Phillip with the mountain man. Or he might be d...." She couldn't say the word.

"But Miss Abby, he wouldn't put out an SOS if Mr. Phillip was, wasn't alive.

Everyone was quiet for the rest of the trip as the helicopter slowly followed the red flag down the mountain. Abby heard sirens in the distance. Soon they would reach the end of the trail. Soon she would see Phillip. Soon she would know one way or the other. She bit her bottom lip and twisted her fingers. Harper laid her head on Abby's shoulder. Soon....

*****

Ken set the copter down on the state road near the end of the trail. Abby ran as fast as Harper to get to the ambulance where they loaded Phillip. He was alive but barely. The medics paused long enough for Abby to speak to him. Phillip rolled his eyes. Did he recognize her? Maybe. Maybe not. She hugged Harper. Phillip was alive. God had told her he was,
but she'd doubted.

"Come, Abby. I'll take you to get your rental car. I know you want to go to the hospital." Ken took her arm assisting her back into the plane.

"We sure do," Harper said, returning to her rear seat.

After going back to the motel and filling a bag with books, a change of clothing, necessities, and snacks, they went to the hospital to wait. Then they each took out their cell phone and called Kentucky.

After several hours, the doctor came into the waiting room to speak with them. He stuck out his hand to Abby. "Hello, I'm Dr. Bledsoe. Are you the next of kin?" Abby swallowed the lump building in her throat. Why? Why would he need the next of kin? Was Pip dying?

"No, but I'm the only one here at the present." He answered her startled look. "It's the law. I can't talk to you. I need permission you can't give me."

"I will soon be his wife. "

Harper raised her eyes. "Really?"

Abby ignored her. She would be, just as soon as he asked her.

The doctor continued, "If the infection travels up his leg any further, we will need to amputate. Can you call the niece and ask her to come? We may need her."

"I'll try, but I'll tell you now, Phillip will never give permission for you to take off his leg."

"That's why I need next of kin. He is in no position to make such a decision."

Abby called Janine's cell phone, only to find she was already on her way. She was driving and would stop in Sevierville for the night and reach Knoxville in the morning. Hopefully, a decision would not be needed before then.

Abby and Harper settled into two reclining chairs for the night. They wouldn't leave Phillip until Janine arrived.

A hot meal and a hot bath summoned Abby and Harper from the motel room as soon as Janine joined them at five in the morning. They gave Abby's cell number to Janine and to the nurse who promised to call if there were any changes, good or bad. Then they went back to the motel to freshen up and sleep a few hours.

"Ah, that felt good." Abby walked to the dresser mirror to brush her hair after a long, hot shower.

It's about time you came back for a rest. Phillip is in the care of some fine nurses. You don't want to get sick, too.

"I thought I left you at home. I don't feel like your nagging tonight." Abby ran her hands over her eyes and yawned.

I'm not nagging. Just wondering why Phillip's plane crashed in Tennessee when he told you he was traveling in
the opposite direction. Is he keeping secrets from you? Do you really want to marry a man who would lie to you about his whereabouts? Do you really?

Abby stared into the mirror glaring back at the short, curly-haired woman. "You can doubt all you want to, but I believe in Pip. I believe in his love for me, and I believe in God.

And lastly, I believe in me. I am worth finding true love. I deserve happiness, and you can't say anything to change my mind. If he didn't tell me where he was going, he had a good reason. This is good-bye to you, sister. From now on, I don't need a doubting Thomas."

Abbigail, that's exactly what I've been waiting to hear you say. So, you love and trust him? Then marry him. No
more doubts.

Abby leaned into the mirror and kissed the face in it. "Thank you. Now I can enjoy whatever Harper's cooking up in there in the microwave."

Harper and Abby slept a few hours before the phone woke them. Janine said Phillip was awake and asking for Abby. Neither of them wasted time getting dressed and going to the hospital. Phillip rolled his eyes and grinned his lop-sided grin when they walked through the door.

Janine explained the infection was responding to the antibiotics, but Dr. Bledsoe held reservations about saving the leg.

Hugs and kisses passed around, Phillip asked Harper and Janine if they minded stepping into the waiting room while he discussed something with Abby.

"Oh sure, I'll just hop on down to the nursery to peek at the new babies."

"We'll have to drag that girl away from that nursery. She's addicted to babies. What is it you wanted to talk about, Phillip?"

"You know I told you I was going to Chicago. Guess by now you realize that's not where I went."

"I presumed you would explain when you were ready." She felt of his forehead to make sure he wasn't over-exerting himself. He was warm, but not hot.

Phillip held her hand. "I found Connie. She's in a nursing home right here in Knoxville. I wanted to check out the P I's report before we got you excited."

"Did she tell you where Cynthia is? How is she? Oh Phillip, thank you." She kissed him three times in succession on his forehead.

"I didn't tell her who I was. Just pretended to be one of the staff. She didn't say much. Harry and I were on our way back to get you when we crashed.

"Phillip, I don't know what to say. We'll go back when you are well enough to visit." Could she really wait that long?

He squeezed her hand. "No, you go now. I'll go back later. We're right here in the same city where she is. I couldn't ask you to go home without seeing her. She might talk to you more than me. I was afraid I'd scare her."

"I'll go today."

"Abby."

"Yes, Phillip."

"Thank you for not questioning why my plane went down in Tennessee, when I told you I was going to Illinois. I know how it must have looked."

"I love you, Phillip, and I believe you love me. Yes, the question entered my mind, but I realized, with love comes faith. I'll never doubt either one of us again."

"I'm so glad, sweetheart." The gold flecks in his hazel eyes danced in circles. Then he grew quieter. "Abby, don't be surprised if she tells us something we don't want to hear. She said something that made me doubt. I asked her how many children she had, and she said she had one, but lost her. That's all she would say. Just turned toward the wall. I wanted to press her, make her answer me, but thought better of it."

"Do you think she's- she's not-not here anymore? What happened? Did she say why?"

"No, she wouldn't tell me more. Go, Abby, and see if you can find out what happened to our daughter."

"I will, Phillip. Do you mind if I leave now? I need to process this information. Janine will be back in here soon. We met her downstairs, getting herself a snack. Harper and I will visit Connie."

"Yes, sweetheart. Go and rest. I am getting tired now." Beads of sweat popped out on his forehead. Abby bent over to kiss him bye. His face seemed warmer. *I'll find our daughter, Pip, if she can be found.*

Abby explained the situation to Harper on the way back to the motel, clarifying she would need to speak to the lady alone.

"Of course, Miss Abby, but if she is that lady who stole your daughter, I sure would like to tell her a thing or two."

"No, Harper, we can't upset her. She's old and not well. Also, if we scare her, she may never tell us about Cynthia?"

"Cynthia? Memaw used to call CeeCee something that sounded like that, but I can't remember."

*****

"Well, looks like we're here. Come on in and say a prayer for me while you wait." Abby pulled the rental car into a parking space for visitors.

When they got inside, Abby asked the receptionist for Connie London's room number, and where Harper might wait.

She gave Abby the number and showed Harper a waiting room. "A young lady is waiting to see her grandfather as soon as he gets his bath. Maybe you can help entertain an irritable infant and a child about two or three."

Abby smiled. Harper would be fine in there, the way she loved children.

Abby slowly walked the short distance across the hall and two doors down. What was she going to say? She pulled at her skirt, brushed back a curly sprig of hair, and stood in the doorway a long minute, not saying a word. She just stood there and watched the frail old lady toss and turn in her sleep. Abby was about to leave when her cousin's eyes opened. "Cynthia is
that you?"

"No, Connie, it's me, Abigail. I've been looking for you and Cynthia for years."

Connie turned her head away from Abby. "No, you're not Abigail. Just a dream."

Abby took her by her shoulders and shook gently. "Connie. Look at me. It's Abigail."

Connie looked at Abby. "Abigail, is it really you? I'm sorry I hurt you. God has punished me for what I did." She stared over Abbey's shoulder toward the door. "But we loved her so much and Brian was scared you'd take her away from us." She pulled the sheet over her face, covering all but her eyes.

"No, Connie, we planned to buy a home in Bowling Green. We hoped we could share her love with you and Brian. I knew what it was like to be separated from my parents; I'd never do that to my child. She must have loved you as much or more than me. We could have all been happy."

Connie turned to Abby. The sadness in her face spokes tons. Abby needed to know; yet could she handle the answer? Her heart pounded until her ears rang. At last,

she would know what happened to Cynthia. "Where is she, Connie? You promised I could have her back."
"She's gone, Abigail. Gone."
Reluctant to ask, Abby stared blankly before the question burst out. "Why—what happened? What do you mean, *gone?*" Abby sat motionless, awaiting the reply, but deep inside, she knew what Connie was about to say. Cynthia was dead. *Oh, Phillip you should be here with me.*
Finally, Connie said, "Accident. She was in the car wreck. Head went through the windshield." Connie's sallow complexion showed her age. Her hands shook, and her skin hung loose from her small frame. She must be at least eighty by now. She appeared in her late nineties. Hiding a child for all those years with the fear of Abby finding her, must have taken its toll. But Connie and Brian had legal authority to keep Connie. Abby didn't understand.
"Abigail, I'm tired now. I need sleep." She turned toward the pale green wall and snuggled under the handmade cover without giving Abby an answer. Muttering unrecognizable sentences. The words made no sense. "'Hide. Keep moving. Jail.' Brian said." Connie withdrew into her own little world, leaving Abby standing on the outside.
"What did you say? I can't hear you?" Abby asked, but Connie continued muttering. Abby understood something like, "Should have never let her go to school up north. Bad things happen when people mix ..."

A sweet refrain wafted down the hall from toward the waiting room. Connie sat straight up in bed. "Who is singing? Am I dreaming?"

"No, you're not dreaming. That's Harper. She sings that lullaby to any baby she can cuddle."

Connie's trembling hands bounced the covers. "Harper? Abigail, why are you doing this to me? Do you hate me so much, you're seeking revenge?" She turned her back to Abby. "There I go dreaming again. I hear Cynthia's sweet voice singing her little song in my dreams. Gotta sleep now. My medicine helps me sleep, but I hate the dreams." Abby got no more responses from Connie. She dreaded going back to Phillip with little more information than he had already garnered.

But there was something more. Some pieces of this puzzle didn't fit. Maybe Phillip would figure it out when he was better. Why did Connie get upset over mentioning Harper's name? Like she said, must be the medicine. She hastened back to the hospital to be with the man she loved.

When Abby and Harper reached the hospital, Dr. Bledsoe met them in the hallway. Mr. Barnes and his niece gave me permission to discuss his case with you. Ms. Fitzgerald, do you believe in miracles?"

"Of course, I do. Has something happened we need a miracle?" Abby's eyes bulged.

He laughed. "No, it's the other way around. I would have staked my reputation; we'd have to amputate that leg. If
I didn't believe in miracles, I do now. Just wait until you see him. He's yelling to go home."

Abby's whole face lit into a smile, as did Harper's.

"Home? When?" Abby asked. Harper squeezed Abby's waist and giggled.

"Hey," he said, "you three sure are antsy. If that leg heals as much by tomorrow as it did in the last twenty-four hours, we can release him tomorrow after we read the results of his blood work. Now remember. As soon as you get him home, I want him seen by a wound care specialist." He handed Abby a prescription, so she could have the wheelchair waiting for him at his release.

Chapter 23

"Sure, feels good to be out of the hospital. Do you think we can stop by the Knoxville Senior Care Residence Home and see Connie?" Phillip asked while Harper pushed him down the ramp to the car.

Abby, one jump ahead of him, answered. "The doctor said we could for a short time but keep the bandage on. Don't touch anything, and all of us need to wash our hands well when we leave. You never know what germs hang around the cleanest of facilities."

Harper and Abby loaded the rental car. Ken offered to fly Phillip home, but he insisted his family would take perfect care of him.

Phillip pulled his cell phone from his pocket. "Think I'll call the Misfits, put them on the speaker, and we can tell them, I'm coming home. Try out this blue tooth. Might have it installed on my car."

The conversation filled with excited ohs, awes, and happy tears, it took Abby several minutes before she could get their attention to ask why Chloe was not answering her phone.

"Went back to that no-good hoodlum she was married to; that's what," Aracella answered. "I'd like to take my rolling pin to his—"

Abigail Fitzgerald for once opened her mouth but remained silent.

Madison finished Aracella's sentence. "Chloe swears Troy has changed. Since he was a model prisoner, his parole officer helped him use the mechanical engineer's degree he earned in prison to get a good paying job as a diesel mechanic, and the courts gave them a trial award custody of Wally."

Abby clenched the steering wheel. "I hope she knows what she's doing. That man didn't look like a changed man to me."

"People can change, and Chloe lit into him like a hammer to a nail when he first come home. Can't blame a man for taking up for himself."

Abby didn't correct her language this time. She just shook her head. "It takes a lot to change people like that."

Harper dropped her head. "I changed."

Madison, still on the phone, said, "Yes, sweetie, you did."

"I'm sorry, Harper. You've changed into a different young lady from that wild teenager who came into my place looking for a job. But let's get back to Chloe. I can't help thinking she's making a big mistake. But then I can't expect
to win them all."

"Don't beat yourself up, Abby. You have to expect
one to fall through the crack now and then." Phillip curled the pillow around his neck in the back seat.

"I know, but it still hurts."

"Like I said, we gotta hope Troy will be good to her this time, and she did get Wally back." Harper reached into
the back seat and straightened Phillip's blanket.

"I know, but I don't trust that man."

"Neither do I," Aracella spoke through the blue tooth car speakers.

"We'll talk about it when we get home. I must keep my mind on driving, or we might get some blue bruises when
I roll this car down the side of a mountain." They all laughed, and Abby disconnected. "It's nice to be able to keep both hands on the wheel and still use the phone, but it gets difficult to keep my mind on news like that and the road at the same time."

They stopped by the nursing facility before heading home, "Do you want me to wait in the lobby?" Harper asked when Abby parked the car.

"Just for a few minutes, Harper. Remember what we discussed?"

"Yes, Miss Abby, but I still don't understand why."

"I don't either, dear, but something is amiss, and hopefully, we can get to the bottom of it. I called the nurse, Ms. Karen Atterbury, to see if Connie was up to visitors today and she told me something that made my skin quiver."

"What did she tell you?" Phillip asked.

Abby wrinkled her brow. "I'm not sure. Just said she needed our help with another patient and wanted Harper to sing that song again. I have no idea what she wants."

Harper pushed Phillip to the waiting area and Connie nodded at the nurse, who followed down the hall to Connie's room.

Connie's eyes opened, but she quickly closed them.

"Hello, Connie. Glad you're awake. I enjoyed seeing you the other day. Hope we can chat again." She hoped Connie would tell her some answers. Had her senility gone too far?

"Huh? Then that wasn't a dream?" Connie opened her eyes and crinkled her face. "Were you really here? Thought I was dreaming. Did I hear Harper? Did I say anything?"

"Do you know Harper?" Abby glanced at the open door, her fingernails digging creases in the palm of her other hand.

Harper's soft voice sang the same lullaby as before. "I'm not dreaming now, am I? You said it was Harper. I remember."

Harper came in the doorway still singing. She took one look at the lady in the bed and pitched the blanket in the air. "Memaw! Is that you Memaw?"

"Harper? You've grown up." Connie closed her eyes again and covered her complete face with the sheet.

Harper's wild eyes settled on Abby. "I don't understand. My Memaw is your Connie?"

Phillip rolled himself inside the door. "We are all confused, Harper, but try singing your lullaby again. Maybe we can get an answer."

Abby sat in the chair quietly, but all sorts of puzzle pieces filled her head tight as a helium balloon. If only the pieces fit together.

Harper cuddled the blanket and sang the old Welch lullaby. *"Cus-ga dee vur mh-lent-in tloose Cus-ga -"*

When she reached the next part, an identical soprano swelled from down the hall, joining her with *"dee vur mh-lent-in tloose-, Cus-ga dee vur mh-lent-in tloose."* Two indistinguishable voices intermeshed as one. Abby clutched her heart and grabbed Phillip's hand. "Oh dear, Jesus!"

Harper turned toward the singing voice, and tears rolled down her eyes. "Cee Cee. That's my Cee Cee's song." Connie turned toward the window and closed her eyes.

Harper repeated the song and so did the voice down the hall. Harper, still singing held out her hands for Abby and Phillip.

Together they followed the nurse, whom Abby had spoken to earlier, toward a room in the psychiatric section just down the hall. "I tuned on the inter coms to both rooms," the nurse whispered.

Abby rolled Philip behind Harper. Phillip placed his hand over Abby's on the handle of the chair. "Are you up to this, sweetheart? No telling what we are about to encounter."

"Yes, as much as you are, I assume. Let's just get inside that room." She asked Harper to continue singing the lullaby she had sung to Cynthia when she was a young child. Who would be singing it now? She hoped whoever it was could tell her where she learned it. Maybe that person could lead her to Cynthia.

They stepped inside the door and Abby nearly collapsed onto the wheelchair atop Phillip. Harper grabbed her and held her up. The woman turned her hazel eyes toward the visitors and ran her fingers through her dark, curly hair. Phillip breathed hard and squeezed

MsFitZ CAFE

Abby's hand. "That's her. It has to be. Don't scare her. She's probably afraid of us."

Abby gulped and whispered. "It's her, Phillip. It's Cynthia."

Harper started to shake. "What is it Harper? Don't worry about me, I'm fine." Abby hugged her, but Harper paid no attention to Abby. Her eyes locked on Cynthia. She began to sing again, and the lady followed her. Harper stepped toward the rocking chair, fell to her knees, and put her head in Cynthia's lap. Harper raised her hand and touched Cynthia's face. "CeeCee. My CeeCee."

Cynthia patted Harper's head, "Baby. Sweet little fhlentyn."

Abby gasped. Phillip's hand trembled under hers. Oh, *dear Jesus, what is this? Is Harper Cynthia's daughter? She can't be.*

Harper raised her tear-filled eyes to meet Abby's and Phillip's. "Memaw and Gramps told me she was dead." Harper whispered. "She's my momma. Did you know Cynthia is my momma?"

"No, Harper, we didn't know. We suspected something odd after the first visit, but not this. Nothing like this. We never dreamed you're our granddaughter." Abby
held out her arms to Harper.

"Granddaughter? I'm your granddaughter! You—you're my Grandparents." She ran back to Cee Cee. "I have a momma and real grandparents. Oh, praise Jesus. I have family."

Still afraid of upsetting their daughter, Abby and Phillip sat quietly for several minutes, showing no outward emotions, but inside, every nerve in Abby's body tensed. The hair follicles of Phillip's arm expanded under her hand. Abby walked to Cynthia's chair and touched her face as she did many years ago and sang the Welch lullaby to her daughter. Cynthia looked all around as if trying to find someone. She tilted her head and listened. Then her eyes met Abby's. "Mabby?"

Abby's heart lurched against her chest. "Mabby." How long had it been since she'd heard that sweet word? She'd never expected to hear it again.

Tears rolling, heart pumping, and fingers trembling, Abby took her Cynthia in her arms. "Yes, sweetheart, it is Mabby." Happy tears overflowed. "There's someone else here who wants to meet you, if you feel up to it."

Like closing a gray curtain over Cynthia's eyes, they faded into a blank stare. "I don't know him." She wrapped her arms around herself and sank bank in her chair, withdrawing from Abby and the people around her, back into her quiet world. The nurse asked them to let her rest for a while. Phillip's time would come later.

They said their unacknowledged goodbyes. In the hallway, Phillip turned to the nurse. "We'll be back, and the next time we'll take her with us. I'm very tired now, but I
have many questions to ask. Can you give me the name of the facility's administrator? We'll be moving our daughter to Kentucky. My attorney will work out all the details and perhaps find us some answers." He handed her his business card, and she gave him one of the administrator's cards from her desk.

Abby leaned against Phillip's chair and took a deep breath. The nurse asked if she was all right. Abby didn't answer but asked her own question. "Why didn't you tell us she was here?"

"I didn't know for sure she was the one you were looking for, and none of the last names matched. Besides, I'm not allowed to give information about any of the residents. I thought if I got all of you together, the mystery would work itself out."

"Does Connie know Cynthia is here? Do you know how to contact Brian London?"

"No to both questions. A gray-haired gentleman admitted Cynthia and arranged with the administrator. Connie came in later. You will need to speak to Dr. McElroy for more information. As I said, there's some kind of mystery going on as I don't find contact information on file for either of these ladies. We were instructed to contact Dr. McElroy, our administrator, if they needed anything."

Phillip leaned on the arm of his chair, his wan face indicating he was becoming weak.

Abby touched the nurse's arm. "We can never thank you enough for what you've done and hope you have not brought trouble on yourself by helping us."

"I'm glad if I helped. This lady needs more than what she's receiving here. I may lose this job, but it will be worth it."

Phillip whispered to Abby and she, in turn, spoke to Ms. Atterbury. "If you lose your job, please call us. Cynthia will need a private nurse for a long time. Or if you prefer not to relocate, we are able to help, and assure you will be financially taken care of."

"Oh, no. I don't want money. I just needed to do what was right."

"We will discuss this later. Right now, my friend here is extremely ill, and we must go now, but we'll be back."

With shaky hands, Phillip handed Abby another one of his business cards and nodded toward the nurse. Abby
gave her the card and asked her to call if there were any changes at all. She wanted to learn more about that man who dropped off her daughter, but Phillip needed to rest. There would be time after Phillip recovered. They had found their daughter. The explanations would come later. The detectives had more information now. Brian would be found.

When the three settled back into the rental car, Harper's face lit as only Harper's face could. "You know, now that you have a daughter and a grandkid, you gonna have to get married. It just wouldn't be right if you didn't."

"I think you are right, Harper." Phillip winked at Abby.

"I agree." Abby smiled almost as wide as her granddaughter."

The family of three returned to Bullitt County. Janine insisted Phillip stay with her until they could get him into rehab.

"I can take him every day if need be." Abby told Janine.

"Thank you, Abby, but we'll have to get him in to see a specialist first and go from there. Meanwhile, Uncle Phillip can stay with me, and, Abby, you can come and visit him as often as you like. I'll be at work every day. He'll need someone to check on him." She put her arms around her uncle's neck and tickled the moustache he'd been growing since the crash. "You'd like that wouldn't you Uncle?"

I always want to see Abby, but I can take care of myself."

"Sounds just like a man." Abby pretended to pout. "I was all ready to nurse him and spoil him with chicken and dumplings every day. Now he doesn't even want me."

Phillip spoke quickly. "Nobody said I didn't want the spoiling part of that deal."

They laughed, and Abby suggested she and Harper leave and let Phillip get some rest. He insisted they pretend tomorrow was Wednesday and bring him some of those dumplings.

"Uh, Mr. Ph—, I mean Grandpa, Oh, you are just going to have to tell me what to call you. I wanted to say, tomorrow *is* Wednesday." They got a good chuckle out of that before the two left to see what was happening at the MsFitz Café.

The gang would meet at the café. Too much to tell to convey over a cell phone. They were all there waiting when Abby and Harper arrived—all but Chloe.

Hugs and happy smiles filled the room. "Aracella pulled Harper close and squeezed her into a hug. "Now I know why Ms. Abby was so attached to you. And Harper, I'm glad you got a real family."

"Me, too, Aracella, but I already had me a rather good one, right here in this room. I just didn't have sense enough to realize it. Now I have a larger one." She stood still and quiet for as long as fidgety Harper could. She twirled around and nodded. "I got me a cousin, too. It just now dawned on me. Janine is my cousin! Oh my. Wonder if she's thought about that? What if she doesn't want to claim kin to me? You know I'm not like her."

"Harper, you know Janine better than that."

"I know, Ms. Abby, but sometimes I get worried about things."

"We'll have no more of that Miss Abby stuff. Thought I was Gam5maw."

"Guess I'll have to study on that one to get the right word." She scratched an eyebrow.

They talked and laughed some more. "The bistro is coming along fine. I am so proud of you girls." Abby commented on the construction of MsFitz. Harper allowed Abby to get in a few words of what happened in the mountains, however, Harper called all dibs on describing Mountain Man, Jax, with his long white hair that he might near stepped on, and how he was big as three men standing on top of each other.

Madison had been sitting with her hands folded under the table. "Miss Abby are you and Mr. Phillip planning to get married here in the bistro?"

"I don't think so, Madison. I don't think we plan to wait long enough for the workers to finish it."

"Well then, I hope you don't mind if Hal and I do?" All eyes sped to Madison's ring finger as she waved it in the air.

Oh's and Ahs shouted throughout the group simultaneously. Harper wisecracked, "Not so much noise or someone will call the cops."

"I hope so." Madison said. Hugs and kisses, good wishes, and laughter kept the ladies centered on Madison for a long while. But eventually, Abby mentioned Chloe. "I hoped she'd be here to help us celebrate."

"I forgot to tell you. They moved to a little town down south of here. That's where his job is and why Chloe quit. Don't feel bad, Miss Abby, you did your best. We all owe you our lives. Chloe, too." Aracella answered.

Abby brushed a tear with a napkin. "You girls are like my children. I'll always be around with open arms if one of you stray and want to come home."

"We know," they chorused.

"For now, I'm on my way to Janine's place to see my fiancé. I'll give him Madison and Hal's good news. We have a wedding to plan. Two of them!"

Chapter 24

Like a Ferris wheel at a fair, the last few weeks had spun fast, up, down, and around again. Now, autumn, in its final stages, was about to shed all her colorful leaves and fade bare-limbed into Kentucky's unpredictable winter climate.

Abby propped her foot on the ottoman and rested her head against the headrest of the rocker-recliner. She could fall asleep easily, but she should keep her mind busy. So many things needed attention. Cynthia. They must find a proper convalescent home for her while she re-adjusted to life. She and Phillip hoped their daughter, with the proper care, would soon be able to finish her convalescing at home with them.

Abby wanted to take her little girl in her arms and make everything all well like she used to. But Cynthia was no longer a little girl. Not in reality, anyway. The doctors with whom she and Phillip had consulted agreed their daughter would be better-off in a rehabilitation facility until she could reconcile with her family again. Too much change, too soon, could cause trauma, and the good Lord knew Cynthia didn't need more trauma in her life.

At least, now, Abigail had hope. A few months ago, she had no hope and not a bit of forgiveness in her heart. Now, thank God; now, she had it all. And would have even more when Phillip was able to stand beside her in front of the minister. She didn't care if he was in a wheelchair, or if she had to carry him, but Phillip had his pride.

The buzz of Phillip's cell phone broke into Abby's musing. Normally, she wouldn't answer his phone, but the physical therapist still worked with Pip in the other room, and most importantly, the name, Karen Atterbury popped up on the caller ID screen. Abby hastily reached for the phone, but a shiver trembled inside her. Slowly, she clicked the phone icon.

"Hello, Phillip Barnes' cell phone," she answered,

"Mrs. Barnes, this is Karen Atterbury, the nurse you met at the Knoxville Senior Care Home."

Abby felt the warmth of the flush on her cheeks. "This is Abigail Fitzgerald, soon to be Mrs. Barnes."

"Oh, I'm so sorry. I-I thought you were—"

"That's all right. How is Cynthia? Is something wrong?"

Karen Atterbury's answer jolted Abigail into an upright position. Cynthia was fine, but the senior care facility was closing. Cynthia needed to be moved immediately. She informed Abby the State had investigated and ordered all residents relocated.

"Then we will be there tomorrow," Abby said.

"Ah, Ms.—"

"Just call me Abby, Karen. It's not like we have just met. I owe you so much. Now tell me what you wanted to say."

"I suggest you bring your attorney with you. I believe Cynthia's adopted father has power of attorney over her. I'm not sure what you will need to get your daughter out of this place, but I am sure you should get her as soon as possible before the State takes over. Cynthia could get lost in a blanket of paperwork again."

Abby agreed and promised to see Karen the next day.

"One more thing, Abby. No one realizes I have called you. As far as everyone here knows, only the administrator can contact Cynthia's family. I hope you'll keep this confidential. Another position will be hard to obtain if this one gives me bad references, and I'll definitely be looking for another placement soon."

"Don't you worry, dear. We'll see no harm comes your way. Not after what you've done for us."

Karen continued, "But you don't know that man. If Mr. McElroy knew I went behind his back and did the things I've done lately, he'd fire me now to keep me from drawing unemployment benefits and not give me commendations for another nursing job either."

Abby assured Karen neither she nor Phillip would do anything to compromise her employment. Then an idea fell into place. She would need to discuss it with Phillip, of course, but they would need help with Cynthia. If Karen were interested in moving to Kentucky, they could definitely help her. Abby and Phillip would employ her to take care of Cynthia. Or, if she didn't want to permanently live here, they could hire her to accompany Cynthia during the trip to Kentucky and finance her relocation wherever she wanted to go. Reiterating how much they appreciated what she had already done for their family, Abby made Karen the offer, promising her she would not go uncompensated either way.

"We know, Karen, that nothing we can give you will repay you forgiving us back our Cynthia. But I assure you, we will do anything to protect your career and your financial security,"

"Thank you, Abby, but I only did what I felt was my Godly duty. I can't accept any payment. There's no way I could do that."

When Karen refused to accept financial gifts, Abby went back to her first suggestion. "Then you must come to work for us. We're good people, Karen, and will pay you top salary for your help with Cynthia. I know she would be happier with you taking care of her than strangers."

Such a journey into a new life and even the trip to Kentucky, itself, would confuse and traumatize Cynthia. She was already familiar with Karen. This could be good for everyone. They ended the call with Karen agreeing to think about the proposals. This autumn would surely slip away into a perfect winter.

Phillip stood, leaning on his cane in the doorway. Abby looked up. "You heard?"

"Yes, and I'm glad you offered Karen the job."

"Then why such a long face?"

Philip explained to Abby it wasn't that he was unhappy Cynthia would be coming home early, but he was concerned about the power of attorney, plus no one knew where Brian lived, or how hard he would fight to keep her away from them. He would, indeed, get in touch with his attorneys. They would fly to Knoxville today. Hopefully, they could find a loophole, or something, anything to get Cynthia to Kentucky as soon as possible.

Abby stood on her toes and put her arms around Phillip's neck.

. "You know, I once frowned upon your wealth, Pip, but I recant. We would never have seen our daughter without your resources."

"Abigail, I've never flaunted my money. I try to use it wisely. I'm still a simple country boy at heart." Phillip's attempt to lighten the conversation worked. Abby giggled.

"I know, Pip, I know. But I thank God for you and your money."

"Abby," He held her close. There's something else we might want to consider. What about Connie?"

"Connie?"

"Yes, you know Cynthia thinks of her as her mother, and by all legal rights, she is her mother. We could probably get Cynthia released more easily if Connie came also."

"Oh." Abby placed her hand over the tic in her jaw. "You're right. Cynthia would adjust better if she could be

near Connie. Would you do that, Phillip? Would you bring

her back to Kentucky?"

"Do you think we can find it in our hearts not to be bitter toward Connie? It'll be hard, but I'll do anything for Cynthia. I love her. I loved her from the moment you told me about her."

Abby winced. "I'm so sorry I kept her from you." Could Abby do this? She must. "Yes, I agree, bitterness would only confuse Cynthia. Do you think we can put it behind us? Can I pretend she didn't steal my child away from me? Away from us?" She shook her head. "I don't know."

"Abigail. it's time we stop looking back and look toward the future."

"I know that, but--."

"Abby, if we want our daughter to heal and come all the way home, we have to forgive Connie. She took her away, now we will find a way for her to help get Cynthia home."

"You're right, and I promise if I can't end the resentment, I'll never let it show. Cynthia will never be aware of my bitterness."

"You must let it go, Abby. You must for all our sakes. We've each learned much about blaming and forgiving. Now we'll put it into practice."

"Agreed." She could do this. Abby was sure she could.

She did as Phillip suggested. Abby and Harper flew to Knoxville by themselves. Phillip remained in Kentucky, so he might make arrangements for their daughter, make calls to his private investigators, and anyone else including the Knoxville Senior Care. Abby's fiancée, Phillip J. Barnes, would get all his ducks in a row before Abby and Harper went to the residence home.

As was planned, two attorneys met Abby and Harper at the airport.

"Miss Fitzgerald and Harper? I presume. I'm Gerald Roswell, and this is Kevin Kinard, Phillip Barnes' attorneys." They extended their hands. Mr. Barnes insisted we meet you here. We can have some brunch and discuss what we've accomplished, then we'll escort you to your hotel"

Abby shook hands with the lawyers and nudged Harper do to the same. "Glad to meet you, gentlemen. Phillip explained you'd be here waiting. I'm sure if Phillip has confidence in you, that you will do your best to help us. Is there anything I can do?"

Mr. Roswell answered. "There is if you don't mind. Both of you. We need you to pay a friendly visit to Mrs. London. See if she has any idea about the location of her husband."

Anxious to get to Cynthia, Abby barely tasted lunch. She signed some forms and legal papers, then gave the attorneys Cynthia's original birth certificate, before they dropped her and Harper at the hotel.

After checking into their rooms, Abby and Harper took a cab to the rest home, where they met Karen at her desk, and she joined them in Connie's room. Luckily, she was awake, and reached out to Harper.

Abby greeted Connie with a smile and a hug. "I brought Harper to see you. We had no idea she was your granddaughter. Never knew Cynthia was married, or Harper existed. Can you and Brian explain any of this to us?"

Connie pushed up with her elbows. "Abigail, forgive me please. Brian told me you had changed your mind and wanted to take her away from us. He said we had to run with her. Said you refused to ever let us see our little Cindy again. He showed me a letter from you."

"I never wrote that letter, Connie.

"I know that now. Brian lied to me about everything. He confessed to me several years after it was too late."

"Where is he now? I need to talk with him. We want to take Cynthia home with us. We've found a doctor who believes he can help her. And Connie, Phillip and I want you to come, also."

"I want you to come, too." Harper leaned over Connie's bed and kissed her forehead Connie continued as if she didn't hear either of them. "He told me Cynthia died in the accident and Harper would be better off with her daddy's folks than with us."

Harper squinted. "You told me Cee-Cee died, I wanted to see her, and you told me she burned in the fire with Daddy. Why? Why did you do that? You had to know."

"No, Harper. I didn't know. He said there was nothing left of my precious girl, and he took care of everything." Tears rolled from Connie's eyes. "I don't know where he is. Haven't seen or heard from him since he dropped me off here." Connie withdrew into herself again and turned to the wall. Karen pulled a blanket around Connie's shoulders.

Abby took her cell phone from her purse. "Hello, Phillip." She listened as Phillip told her the news. The detectives and lawyers had worked all night and into the morning, comparing notes, speaking with police enforcement, and seeking the aide of some judges. In layman terms, they told Phillip that Brian had learned the finance company he worked for in Bowling Green was laundering money through their business. Brian manipulated the computers and stole $750,000.00. That is when he took Connie and Cynthia away in their motor home. They home-schooled Cynthia and traveled north until Cynthia started high school. Then they switched states every school year until she went to college.

"Abby's eyes rounded. "Where is he now?"

"Not sure, but my guys suspect he's in protective custody with a new identity. Seems as if he disappeared after testifying at the trial. Several mafia members and the owners of the finance company were arrested, tried, and found guilty. But you know there must still be mafia out there searching for Brian. The Kentucky police were obliging, helping us to contact the proper judges and officials who helped us gain guardianship of Cynthia. Of course, they told us they had no idea where Brian London was now."

"Oh my," Abigail shivered at the thought of how Cynthia must have grown up. No wonder she couldn't handle the death of a husband and child. Who could?

"So, when can we take our daughter home with us?" Abby turned on the phone's speaker so Harper would get off her shoulder attempting to eavesdrop on the conversation.

"As soon as you and Karen can get her ready. The company jet is on its way to the airport to pick
you up. Have you spoken to Karen yet?"

Abby looked at Karen questioningly. "Yes, but not sure what she's planning to do."

Karen answered her. "I'm going with you."

"So am I." Connie sat up in bed.

Within the hour the four ladies were on the

MsFitZ CAFE

way to Kentucky.

Epilog

She stood in front of the floor-length mirror and confronted that familiar twin in the looking glass. Her pale ivory gown, plain, simple, and beautiful complimented her from face to floor. The mirror-face whispered, Y*ou are gorgeous, Abigail. You deserve this.*
"I know." Abby smiled. "I thought God was punishing me, but instead He's forgiven me."

The open space in the roof over the herb garden let in the warm, drizzling rain forming the green waterfall. The foliage of the herbal plants lifted their faces and drank from heaven's fountain. Janine and the MsFitz Café staff stepped in rhythm with the jazz music as it flowed around the bridal party marching to the front center of the waterfall. Harper held onto Cynthia's hand, guiding her toward Phillip and Uncle Joey.

From upbeat jazz to strains of "Here Comes the Bride," the jazz band segued. Hal Mainer accompanied Abby past the garden toward the slate wall covered with trickling water, to her place beside Pip. The rain had stopped, and a rainbow appeared in the sky. Abby smiled. She'd found the golden pot at the end of her rainbow, and it was filled with second chances.

She allowed herself one quick glimpse around the Varanese before losing herself in Pip's gold and hazel eyes. Her heart warmed as three latecomers slipped inside the Varanese door. Wally, a handsome little guy in his suit and tie, held Chloe's hand. His other hand rested in Troy's. The three of them wore smiles that spoke louder than the band played. Abby's smile matched theirs. The crack in the floor was closed. She lifted her eyes to Pip.

The minister finished with, "I now pronounce you man and wife, Mr. and Mrs. Phillip Barnes. You may kiss the bride."

END

To my Readers:

Thank you for reading MsFitZ . I hope it added a blessing and pleasure to your life. If you enjoyed this or any
 of the other books, I hope you will go to Amazon.com, or Goodreads and leave a review.

More books by Jean Thompson Kinsey

The Light Keeper's Daughter (soon to come, two more in this series (as of yet untitled)

The Logan County Trilogy: Secrets at Willow Shade, Shadows in the Shade, and Murder at Willow Shade

Riches to Rags

Jean T Kinsey

Run Ruby Run

More Than Blood Reveals

I love hearing from my fans. Email me at kystorywriter@gmail.com or leave a message on Jean's Books on Face Book.
Visit my blog at http//www.kystoywriter.blogspot.com

Website: http//www.kystorywiter2.com to visit "Jean's Clean Books"

Made in the USA
Columbia, SC
05 October 2024